M
Clarke, Anna

Soon she must die

64889

WITHDRAWN

DATE DUE			
OCT 0 9 1984			
NOV 1 4 1984			
DEC 2 0 1984			
JAN 2 8 1985			
APR 1 5 1986			
JAN 2 6 1987			
JUL 2 9 1988			
JAN 1 1 1990			

PUBLIC LIBRARY,
JEFFERSON, IOWA

SOON SHE MUST DIE

By Anna Clarke

SOON SHE MUST DIE
WE THE BEREAVED
DESIRE TO KILL
GAME SET AND DANGER
LETTER FROM THE DEAD
ONE OF US MUST DIE
THE DARKENED ROOM
A MIND TO MURDER
THE END OF A SHADOW
PLOT COUNTER-PLOT
MY SEARCH FOR RUTH
LEGACY OF EVIL
THE DEATHLESS AND THE DEAD
THE LADY IN BLACK
THE POISONED WEB
POISON PARSLEY
LAST VOYAGE

Anna Clarke

SOON SHE MUST DIE

PUBLISHED FOR THE CRIME CLUB
BY
DOUBLEDAY & COMPANY, INC.
GARDEN CITY, NEW YORK
1983

All of the characters in this book are fictitious,
and any resemblance to actual persons,
living or dead,
is purely coincidental.

Library of Congress Cataloging in Publication Data
Clarke, Anna, 1919–
Soon she must die.
I. Title.
PR6053.L3248S6   1983   823'.914
ISBN 0-385-19106-5
Library of Congress Catalog Card Number 83–11497

First Edition

Copyright © 1983 by ANNA CLARKE
All Rights Reserved
Printed in the United States of America

SOON SHE MUST DIE

1

"'Delightful bijou residence,'" read Jane. "'Two reception, two bedrooms, usual offices, utility room, patio with grapevine.'"

"Why?" asked Robert. He moved a pawn on the chessboard and then glanced at the folded newspaper that lay beside the board on the glass-topped coffee table.

"Why what?"

"Why is a patio with a grapevine a selling point. I should think it would darken the windows. I don't see how white can mate in two moves. Black would have to be an imbecile. How much?"

"How much what?"

"How much is the bijou residence?"

"A hundred and thirty-five thousand pounds," replied Jane.

"That's eleven-point-two-five times our combined annual earnings," said Robert without any hesitation.

Jane threw the London *Evening Standard* at him and it knocked the white king off the board. He replaced it without comment, glanced at the newspaper on the coffee table again, and then propped his chin in his hands and stared at the board. In the armchair the other side of the gas fire Jane drew up her legs and hugged her knees and looked across at his bent fair head with an expression of brooding affection on her face.

"It seems so daft for you to be teaching English literature," she said, "when you can work out impossible chess problems and do calculations without even thinking about them. There ought to be some way you could make money out of it."

"I've got a degree in English literature," said Robert. "I'm not qualified to do anything else."

"But nobody wants any Arts graduates nowadays, except grotty tutorial colleges with no prospects at all."

"I don't understand computers and never will," said Robert. "Ah! The knight. Of course. That's neat. Really neat." He stared at the board with great satisfaction for a moment or two before putting the chess-men back in their box. "I'm with you now, love. Are you really hankering after a luxury rabbit hutch with bunches of unripe grapes round the door?"

"Not necessarily, but I should love to have a decent home. I'm sick to death of being poor."

"We're not all that poor. And we're lucky to get anything at all in the middle of London."

"And we're lucky to have enough to eat and we're lucky to both have work and not to be on the dole. I know, I know, I *know!* And I'm sick of it. I'm twenty-seven and you're twenty-nine and in five years' time we'll be just the same as we are now only worse because everything will be even more expensive and there'll be even fewer jobs than ever. I want money. *Real* money. And I want it *now*. I don't want the ground floor flat of a Victorian workman's cottage with a converted coal-shed as a kitchen. Fancy having a coal-shed as a kitchen in nineteen-eighty-two! It's ridiculous. How many people have their kitchen in a coal-shed?"

"I don't know," said Robert, "but we could probably find out from the census statistics. They seem to be obsessed with asking questions about plumbing nowadays."

"Oh, don't be so bloody funny!" cried Jane. "Can't you see I mean it?"

Robert looked up at her and nodded without speaking. He was a large, placid-looking man who looked younger than his years. Jane, when she was feeling frustrated and depressed as she was now, looked older. But when she was happy and hopeful there was a glow and vitality about her that was ageless and timeless and more attractive than any formal beauty. She had red hair and green eyes and an air of barely controlled restlessness, except when she was doing her job, which was nursing, and which she did very well indeed. They had lived together for five years and it was Jane who did not want to get married.

"Not yet," she always said when Robert suggested it. "I don't feel settled enough. Let's wait till we get a decent home."

It hurt a little when she said this, but then she often said things that hurt. Robert never showed that he felt it. Life had given him good training in hiding his feelings. When he was two weeks old he had been found by a policewoman in a public telephone box near Waterloo Station and his home for the next few months had been the Children's Hospital. Doctors and nurses fought for the life of the near-dead infant as if he had been a royal prince, and when they had completed their part of the job the Social Services Department took over.

Fostering, rather than an orphanage, was then very much in vogue, and for the next few years the child played in a small room with a West Indian boy and a Northern Ireland orphan and grew bigger and stronger and learnt to walk and talk but learnt little else. The next foster home lasted for about a year, and it was here that he first began to build up memories of fear and pain. When the foster-mother was struck off the Social Services register, not for her own sins but for those of her alcoholic husband, Robert was moved yet again, this time to a temporary refuge run by a religious community, while the authorities decided what was to be done with him.

It turned out to be the only happy time of his childhood. Sunshine and warmth, grass to run on, rabbits and cats to play with instead of the crowded little house that smelt of fear. Above all, there was a human face. Pale, but with dark hair and eyes that looked straight at him when the voice spoke his name, so that for the first time he knew that he really was Robert, and that somebody else knew it too, and that he would go on being Robert, growing older and stronger day by day.

He never learnt to give the face a name, but he did learn to attach to it a feeling that he later came to realize was love. And when the face and the voice disappeared from his life and he was on the move again—for it was only an emergency solution and there were other children in greater need—he learnt how to feel loss and mourning and despair. And also the art of survival. You must feel nothing: thus you cannot be hurt. You must hope for nothing: in this way you cannot be disappointed. You must build around yourself a shell, a smooth impenetrable shell, with all the rejection and the pain outside, and within it only yourself, isolated but safe.

Such was the survival kit of Robert Fenniman, named after the policewoman who found him and the doctor who was chiefly responsible for saving his life. The mild and placid manner was an essential part of the protective shell. Jane did not realize this, although she often had the feeling that she would never really know him, no more than he would ever know the truth about his origins. She was half-fascinated, half-disturbed by Robert's history, and could not understand how he could be so calm and incurious.

There was nothing mysterious about her own background, but in many ways her life had been almost as unsettled as Robert's. Her father had been an inventor, a wild and freakish man with a touch of genius, constantly going bankrupt and starting over again. Her mother was constantly leaving him and then returning to him again, and she was now spending a contented widowhood in a small South Coast seaside town, keeping house for her bachelor brother and enjoying her gardening and her bridge.

Jane was fond of her in an irritated way, but she always returned from her visits to her mother more restless than ever and complaining about the intolerable narrowness and complacency of her mother's life.

"I suppose your Uncle Walter will leave you some money when he dies," said Robert.

They often had this sort of conversation. Jane had not the slightest idea that her violently expressed discontent touched in him the deepest springs of insecurity and unease.

"Walter's got nothing worth having," said Jane with contempt.

"There's the house."

"Cheap little semi-detached bungalow surrounded by about four hundred others all exactly the same. No thanks."

"You could sell it."

Robert's hand reached out for the red plastic box that held the chess-set. The feel of it comforted him. He went over the solution to the problem in his mind and it brought some comfort. A little bit of firm rock to hold on to while the storm of Jane's passionate and seemingly infinite yearnings beat about him.

"The proceeds of Walter's house wouldn't buy a dog-kennel in London," said Jane predictably. "Not even a coal-shed."

Robert knew better than to suggest they should move out of London. He waited silently, holding tightly in his mind to the subtle beauty of that winning knight's move, while Jane dreamed aloud of impossible splendours. When the lifeline of chess failed him, which it soon would because the storm looked like being the worst he had ever known, he would take refuge in repeating to himself Macbeth's last great speech. "Tomorrow, and tomorrow, and tomorrow . . ." It would bring no comfort, because there was none to be found on these occasions; only black empty horror at the thought of losing Jane. But these heavy bell-tolling lines in his mind would help him to keep calm by measuring and giving rhythm to the hopelessness.

He had got as far as "sound and fury" when the storm blew over at last. Jane came and sat on the floor beside his chair and rubbed her head against his knee like a cat showing its powers of possession.

"I'm sorry, darling." She spoke in a muffled voice.

"I'm sorry too." One hand stroked her hair, the other still gripped the box of chess-men. "There's only one solution I can see to this problem," he went on. Normally on such occasions he would suggest a treat like the best seats at Covent Garden Opera or a weekend in Paris. These frequent "treats," together with books and records and new clothes for Jane, cancelled out what could by now have been quite a big step forward towards the acquisition of a "decent home." Robert had long since learnt that sensible talk about mortgage repayments did not go down well at all. He sometimes suspected that Jane's yearnings were beyond any human satisfaction, but to suggest this to her or to try to disillusion her in any way would put their relationship at risk.

"What's your solution, darling?" asked Jane snuggling closer.

He had meant to say: "We go and have dinner at the Caprice," and he was amazed and appalled at the words that came out instead.

"You must give me up and find a man who can afford to buy you what you want."

It was not only the words. The voice itself sounded different. Harsh, bitter, angry and hurt. A voice that Jane didn't even know existed, that Robert believed had been silenced for ever many years ago. It was as if Macbeth and the chess-men had strained so much to weather the storm that they had ended by breaking his shell. Jane scrambled to her feet and backed away from him, cringing as if he had hit her.

"Do you really mean that? Do you want to get rid of me?"

They stared at each other for a moment, each reflecting the other's horror at the glimpse of the abyss, and then they clung together as if they could never let go.

At the same time the following evening, coming-home and glass-of-sherry time, Jane announced that she had been thinking very seriously and had decided that she must stop nagging Robert and moaning at him and must do something herself about getting hold of more money.

"Don't worry," she added. "I won't do anything illegal. Not identifiably so, at any rate."

"That's a relief." Robert drained his glass and poured out another. It was very easy to lose one's economical habits when one lived with Jane. Before he met her he had been content with little. Or rather, that little had been a lot to him. During the ten years that had followed the loss of the foster-mother who had spoken to him in a voice that gave meaning to his name, Robert had had plenty of opportunities for strengthening his shell. There was no more outrageous ill-treatment, but plenty of insensitivity and lack of affection and encouragement. Then at last, at the age of sixteen, he came into the care of a Quaker couple, both retired schoolteachers. Their unemotional kindness well suited Robert and they also opened up to him the life of the mind.

With their support and guidance he began to read and study and to pass exams. Always very adaptable, always willing to adjust to whatever was required of him provided it did not threaten the Robert within the shell, he soon learnt to appear at home in academic society. His foster-parents were delighted when he was offered a university place, and he was glad for their sake as well as for his own.

Gratitude he could and did feel, but he was incapable of either feeling or showing love. Luckily they did not demand it. Passion of any kind played no part in their quiet house. Gentleness and goodwill; a respect for the individuality of others; a taste for reading and a reverence for truth were the lessons that Robert learnt in the last of his many foster homes.

At college he made many acquaintances but no close friends. Nobody disliked him and nobody cared very deeply about him. He never caused any trouble; wherever he was, he always fitted in. But always he was like an observer, watching the ebb and flow of others' hopes and fears and loves and hates, but never joining in. Avoid strong feelings, for that will save you pain; avoid high hopes, for they can only bring disappointment. The early lessons never failed him. Since he always appeared calm and contented, and never showed any signs of being lonely or unhappy, teachers and fellow-students alike always assumed that his close relationships must be with somebody else.

This detached but not unhappy existence was carried over from the university years into working life. Robert had no aim except to earn his living in a way that would not displease the Quaker couple, and his patience and good humour made him very acceptable as a teacher and as a colleague. He taught English language and literature to a never-ending succession of overseas students, joined in social activities when required, but again formed no close relationship with anybody. Spare time was spent in reading, playing chess, going for long walks alone, and visiting the old couple. He was not conscious of anything lacking, but sometimes, from deep within the shell, a memory stirred of a face and a voice, and then he felt obscurely threatened and would hastily batten it down.

And then, at a party given by one of his fellow-teachers, somebody had introduced him to Jane, and she had burst upon this hermitlike existence like a great blaze of sunshine, bringing it warmth and showing up its sterility. She refused to be put off, as other girls had been, by his air of being friendly but at heart otherwise engaged. She liked him; his seeming invulnerability represented a challenge to her. She loved a challenge. She was determined to make him notice her, to fall in love.

Nothing in Robert's survival kit, nothing in all the lessons that he had learnt from life, had taught him how to stand up against such an onslaught. Attempts to escape only caused the whirlwind to blow the stronger. In the end he no longer wanted to escape, but came out of his sleep of the senses like the earth awakening in spring, and let her take over his life.

And now a life without Jane had become unthinkable and there was no going back. He had broken his own safety code and must pay the price. But oddly enough, close as they were, even Jane had never succeeded in getting through to the Robert within the shell. Perhaps nobody ever would. Perhaps those early hurts had gone too deep for any human heart or mind to heal.

Robert partly understood this and sometimes he felt that there was something lacking between them and that he ought to be more open with her, as open as she always seemed to be about her own life and feelings. He answered her questions about his own history in his usual dispassionate manner but he could never bring himself to tell her about the face and the voice. It was a secret region, too frail and precious to be surveyed by Jane's keen and interested intelligence. She would try to analyse it away, and he would lose something that was in some way even more dear to him than Jane herself.

So there was somehow a gulf between them. Important areas of life and feeling where they were unable to meet.

But for the most part their need for each other enabled them to avoid looking at the gap.

This evening they were both very conscious of the danger and were holding tight to their well-tested positions in an attempt to recover from the previous night's glimpse of the abyss.

"I've never understood how you came to be such a worthy citizen," said Jane affectionately. "It goes against all the rules of sociology. With your upbringing you ought at the very least to have been a problem teenager, and by now you ought to have fully developed criminal tendencies."

"Perhaps I have." He smiled at her.

"No such luck. If there's anything illegal to be undertaken I shall have to do it myself."

"You're not thinking of murdering one of your rich patients, I trust," said Robert lightly.

"Yes, I had thought of that," she replied in the same tone of voice, "but it wouldn't be much use unless I was sure they'd left me a lot of money in their will, would it?"

Her eyes were very bright. She was in a radiant, teasing mood.

"I don't trust you," said Robert. "It's a pity you left the hospital."

"I hadn't much choice after that last row with Matron. And there's a lot to be said for agency nursing. Different surroundings, choose your own hours, and—"

"—rich private patients," interrupted Robert. "I've got it. You're going to worm yourself into the confidence of a senile old lady and go off with her jewellery."

"There's a lot of that going on," said Jane in a more serious tone of voice. "I can understand the temptation, but I'd never do it. It's taking advantage of people's weaknesses when you are supposed to be looking after them. If someone in their right mind likes to give me a present, that's quite different. It's definitely not illegal, I promise you that, and it ought to increase the sum total of human happiness rather than diminish it."

"Am I to be told what it is?"

"Only if it affects you in any way. Not now."

"In that case I'll go and cook our supper. That'll save you from having to go and stand in the coal-shed."

She made a face at him and handed over the bag full of shopping. "It's fillet steak and some pastries from that gorgeous new delicatessen in Hampstead High Street. They sent me on a job up that way today. Tell you about it over supper. I was in a foul mood last night, wasn't I, darling? I'll think up a treat for you to make up for it."

As if I were still a deprived child, thought Robert as he took the food into the kitchen, which was tiny but quite convenient. In fact many a house-hunting Londoner would have envied them their home, which was in a cul-de-sac not far from Paddington Station. The rooms were very small but the conversion was well done; the trains were noisy, but one got used to it, and the middle-aged couple upstairs was friendly but unobtrusive. There were even a few square yards of garden, which had a few hours of evening sunshine in the summer months. Robert's chief worry about it was the fear that their landlord, an elderly eccentric philanthropist, would die and leave them at the mercy of a property company. In which case Jane would have genuine cause for complaint.

He put the meat under the grill and wished for the umpteenth time that Jane could be as happy as he could with bangers and mash. But he knew that this wish had no more hope of being granted than had Jane's longings for limitless luxury. He must accept her dreams and extravagance, just as she must accept the fact that he was never going to earn a lot of money. When you loved someone you had to accept these things. And after all, the miracle, in his case, was not as Jane had supposed that he had grown up law-abiding. The miracle was that with such a childhood as his, he should have dared to love at all. It had been a crazy risk to take, to fall in love, to expose the shrinking creature within the shell to all the destructive forces of the elements. And last night something had cracked a little. Fortunately Jane had realized in time and had quickly helped him to repair the crack.

So now they were going back to where they had been before, never planning for any realizable future, just dreaming (in Jane's case) or taking refuge in the patterns of numbers and chess-pieces (in his own), and arranging little treats for themselves as if they were a couple of unloved children trying to make up to each other for what life had failed to give them.

But we can't go on like this for ever, thought Robert as he tore open the packet of frozen beans; we won't be able to keep on papering over the cracks.

Panic rose again at the thought of a life without Jane. He fought it back, telling himself that it couldn't be quite the same as it had been before last night because nothing was ever quite the same, but different didn't necessarily mean worse. Perhaps Jane was at last beginning to understand something of the effect that these moods of hers had on him. Perhaps she would try to moderate them. In fact, all this chat about getting money from wealthy patients might even be the beginning of such a process. He didn't for one moment believe that she had anything specific in mind, except the very reasonable expectation of receiving a present now and then. But it might take the strain off him a little if her dreaming attached itself to what she thought of as the possibilities of her own situation, instead of coming out as a vague but powerful flow of dissatisfaction that he could not help but feel was partly directed towards himself.

Robert quite enjoyed cooking, and under the influence of these happier thoughts he reached for some tomato and cress to add colour to the meal and yelled to Jane to set the table. This involved moving a pile of books and newspapers and pushing the armchairs nearer to the gas fire.

Jane did this cheerfully, with none of the usual complaints about lack of space and lack of a dining-room.

"Gorgeous grub," she said after they had been eating in silence for a minute or two. "There's your job for when you get sick of teaching. Chefs are always in demand."

Robert could not detect any ulterior motive in this remark so he took it at its face value.

"I wouldn't mind at all, but I believe they expect you to have spent years at a catering college nowadays."

"Not if you're starting up your own little restaurant."

They discussed the pros and cons of this in detail, as if they had capital at their disposal and were seriously considering such a venture. Robert wondered whether it was part of an attempt on Jane's part to show that she too could be realistic about the business of money-making. It seemed to him that some sort of effort from his own side was called for, and he asked her to tell him about the patient in Hampstead, since he had the feeling that she wanted him to.

Jane told him in detail, and Robert forgot about the tensions between them and forgot his own fears. They moved into the armchairs in front of the gas fire to drink their coffee, and Robert watched the play of emotion on Jane's expressive features as he listened to the tragic and very moving human story.

2

Rosamund Morgan was young. Only twenty-five. She was orphaned and she was also very rich, being the only child of a woman who had inherited a large fortune and a man named Benny Morgan, who had built up a chain of supermarkets that had brought him an equally large fortune. She had taken a good honours degree in history and she was a gifted pianist. She was also very beautiful—a dark-eyed, oval-faced madonna.

And she was dying of leukaemia.

Willoughby House was an ugly but well-built late Victorian mansion standing in its own grounds on the edge of Hampstead Heath. Rosamund had been born and brought up there and loved the place. There was no reason why she should have to leave it in order to die.

In charge of the housekeeping was a cousin of her mother's, Mary Warley, who had given up her job as a college catering officer in order to come and live with Rosamund. Bill Warley, also in his early fifties, had at that time no job to give up, but he naturally came along with his wife and was authorized to look after the garden.

The night-time population of Willoughby House included a fourth: a nurse from the agency for which Jane Bates was working. By daytime the population was considerably increased. There was Mrs. Miller who did the cleaning and George who was supervised by Bill Warley; and a variety of nurses from the agency and many regular visitors. Dr. Eric Milton drove his Mercedes between the white stone gateposts at least twice a week, and Mr. Raymond Quick, solicitor, came equally often, not always on business, but as a friend. Other callers included one or two of Rosamund's university friends, and John Aylmer, her first cousin on her father's side.

Mary Warley kept house on a generous scale. Hospitality was never lacking, and were it not for the fact that Rosamund's assets, managed by her father's investment advisers, literally could not fail to keep augmenting themselves, there might have been serious inroads made into the estate, the size of which was a constant source of speculation among all those who lived at or worked at or visited Willoughby House.

Only Raymond Quick knew the contents of Rosamund's will. He was a white-haired, rosy-faced eighty-year-old, in excellent health but long since retired from active partnership in his firm. He retained only the job of trustee of the estate, along with one of the partners, and made it his business to look after Rosamund in every way open to him, just as for many years he had looked after Rosamund's mother. There was very little going on at Willoughby House that Mr. Quick did not know about, but provided it did not threaten Rosamund's peace of mind, he made no comment.

If anything did upset Rosamund, then Raymond Quick would act at once. Up till now it was John Aylmer who was the worst offender in this respect. Rosamund's father had for many years supported his widowed sister and her son John, and Rosamund had kept up the payments, but the son, at any rate, did not regard them as enough. John was quite sure that he could become a second Benny Morgan if only he had the capital to get started, and the total of his failed enterprises rose year by year. Even when she had been strong and healthy Rosamund had found it very difficult to say no. He was, after all, her nearest living relation; he had the features of her father, and one never knew, perhaps next time he really would make a success of it.

In her extreme weakness she was an easy target, and Mr. Quick had to come to the rescue. He had told John that if he mentioned money to Rosamund again, the most likely result would be that he would forfeit his eventual share of the estate, and he didn't want that, did he? No, John agreed, he certainly didn't want that, and it might be better, more decent in fact, to wait, because after all, poor Ros, terribly tragic, cruel irony, with all that she had to live for, etc., etc.

The interview with John had trickled away into the usual clichés. Mr. Quick thought he must have heard about every conceivable variety of reaction to Rosamund's situation. On the whole the younger people, apart from John, were the most tolerable because the most honest. But even from them he never heard the one note that he longed to hear—the note of true, deep, inconsolable grief. Was there nobody but himself who would truly mourn Rosamund? Of course there were plenty who genuinely admired her courage and calm dignity, and of course her college friends would miss her, but that was not what he meant. If only somebody would love her for herself, without any thoughts of her circumstances, and would despair over her loss. What a note that would sound! Mr. Quick felt that that alone would console him, and he knew that if he ever heard that note he would recognize it at once because it would be an echo of his own.

Meanwhile the daily life at Willoughby House went on, and at just about the time when Jane was telling Robert as much as she then knew of Rosamund's story, Mary Warley was sitting by Rosamund's bed in the large ground floor room at the back of the house, which had once been the main sitting-room but that now, for Rosamund, measured the extent of her home.

The curtains were not drawn across the long windows because Rosamund liked to see the last of the daylight. Her view was of an upward sloping lawn containing a scatter of yellow crocuses and daffodils, a copper beech tree, and a high wall of shrubs beyond.

When the last flush of pink had disappeared from behind the bare beech twigs Rosamund said: "Thanks for indulging me, Mary. You must be longing to switch the light on."

"I don't mind sitting in the dark," was the reply. "It's rather restful after all the coming and going we've had today."

Rosamund reached out a hand for the bedside lamp. It lit up the broad, firm-featured face and short coarse grey hair of her cousin. Mary blinked and got to her feet.

"Better draw the curtains. Bill swears that nobody could possibly get through all those holly bushes and burglar alarms round the premises but I feel happier if I feel I've shut them out. Rather ostrichlike, I suppose."

"Curtains," said Rosamund reflectively. "In one sense they are cosy and comforting and in another sense they're scary because there might be something behind them."

She's talking like this more and more, thought Mary Warley; philosophizing over little commonplace things; no longer takes any interest in the news; the horizons come ever closer. There wouldn't be any more remissions now. It was just a question of time. Three or four months? Probably less.

It was not that she actually wanted the girl to die, she told herself. She was just doing her job. When Rosamund died she would sell the house under Mr. Quick's instructions —they worked well together, she and Mr. Quick, each respected the other's efficiency. Then she would give herself a long holiday, perhaps a round-the-world cruise, and then look for a house and a job, for she needed to occupy herself. Bill could come along if he liked, but it would be marvellous if he did decide to take himself off at last. Perhaps out of Rosamund's bequest she could make him a big enough allowance to tempt him to go. Now if Rosamund's death were to mean that she could shake herself free of Bill . . .

Mary Warley's thoughts trudged along their well-worn path while with the surface of her mind she listened to what Rosamund was saying.

"I liked that new nurse they sent this afternoon. The redhaired one. Her name's Jane. She's different. Interesting. Do you think we could have her again, Mary? Or would Caroline be offended?"

"If you want Jane you shall have her. I'll tell the agency to send her tomorrow. In what way is she different and interesting?"

If Bill will go, Mary was thinking, I'll buy a flat. A penthouse in Brighton. And perhaps I won't take a job. Perhaps I'll start a little restaurant there. It'll be a new challenge.

"She chatted about herself," Rosamund was saying, "but then they all do. I suppose it's a sort of defence against the patient's illness. Or perhaps they are told to do it to take the patient out of herself."

She smiled as she said this, and Mary, pulled for a moment out of her own hopes and dreams, wondered not for the first time at the strength and beauty of that pale face. Perhaps it was the eyes, still intensely alive, that produced this extraordinary effect. Mary was not imaginative, but she could not help but feel it.

"But I liked her chat," went on Rosamund. "It wasn't the usual stuff about their husbands and their boy-friends and their incredibly gifted children. She talked about her father, who seems to have been a bit mad but not in the least boring, and about a friend of hers who seems to have had a very deprived childhood but had grown up without any resentment or bitterness or kicking against his fate. I found that very interesting."

"Yes," said Mary thoughtfully, her mind still on Rosamund and not on her own prospects, "I can see that you would. I'll go and ring the agency straight away. They've got a night service. Will you be all right if I leave you? The night nurse hasn't come yet."

"Of course I'll be all right. I can even stagger to the commode if I have to. Sometimes I really wonder whether I need all this nursing."

Rosamund raised herself on one elbow and smiled at her cousin again. She was wearing a dark red dressing-gown because she hated bedjackets, and the sheets were lemon yellow and the bedspread apple green. Yet the sick girl's face was able to hold its own with all this colour. The hair was dark and straight and nothing could ever take away the expression in those eyes.

She's had a good day, thought Mary. It goes up and

down. For one extraordinary moment she had the illusion that Rosamund was not dying at all but simply going through a very long convalescence. The notion that Rosamund might get better was so unthinkable that Mary's mind rejected it almost immediately. But the thought had been there and her reaction to it had shown her something of herself that she would rather not have seen. It just was not true that she looked on her role in this house purely as a job. She really did want Rosamund to die. It was a shattering revelation and it would take a lot of digesting.

"Ring the bell if you want anything," she said. "I'll go and fix up about the nurse now."

When she had left the room Rosamund lay back and thought about her. Poor Mary. So efficient and so convinced that she was never giving away anything that she was feeling or thinking. And yet so transparent, at any rate to Rosamund herself. But they were all transparent: they were all just waiting.

Except Raymond Quick. He would be coming tomorrow morning and they would talk about her mother. And if Mary managed to get the new nurse in, then Mr. Quick would meet her. Rosamund felt a little upsurge of anticipation. It would be interesting to hear what the two of them made of the other.

Jane Bates. A plain and ordinary name. But a far from ordinary girl. The starched uniform only heightened her individuality. No wonder she couldn't work in a hospital. Rosamund smiled again at the account of the row with the matron. And the father, with his passion for Wittgenstein and his chemical experiments that blew up the tool-shed.

Of course the girl might be making it all up, but that didn't matter. It needed imagination to tell that sort of lie, and Rosamund's present existence was starved of imagination. How about the friend, Robert? Was he really "just a friend"? Well, that didn't matter either. Rosamund felt sure that he really existed. She had been watching Jane carefully when she talked about him and had recognized genuine puzzlement when Jane had said that she didn't understand him at all.

"But one simply has to accept the slings and arrows of outrageous fortune," Rosamund had said. "Look at me. What good would it do to be moaning every second about the fact that I am dying?"

"It might keep you alive longer," replied Jane. "Anger is a great healer and strengthener."

Rosamund was fascinated. Nobody ever talked to her like this; not even her college friends. Nobody had the courage. But this little red-haired nurse, who looked quite plain and dull one moment and at the next moment looked like a wild and windblown sunset, seemed to have courage for anything. A touch of the madness of genius, perhaps, like her crazy father.

"You're a fighter yourself, aren't you?" she said.

"Yes," said Jane, "but I know when to stop and wait for the right moment. I can be patient if need be."

"What are you fighting for?"

"Oh—everything. Freedom. No limits. I have the wildest ambitions. Actually I don't think I really know what I want."

"But you won't be happy till you have it."

They smiled at each other.

"Will you come again?" asked Rosamund. "I'd very much like you to."

"I'd love to," said Jane.

"And perhaps sometime you might be able to bring your friend Robert. I'd like to meet him."

Jane looked doubtful. Rosamund said, a little sadly: "You don't think he would care to visit such an invalid? People do tend to find it embarrassing."

"Oh no, no. It's not that. He'd be fascinated to talk to you. You could have a terrific conversation about not kicking against your fate. It's just that—well, it's me, Miss Morgan. You see I'm completely hooked on him, but he's very critical of me, and he'll be even more critical of me after he's met you."

Rosamund laughed out loud. It was a long time since that sound had been heard in the room.

"That somebody can actually be afraid I might steal their man! Me! Oh, this really is blissful. Give me a drink, Jane. I mustn't start coughing. Bless you. I'm so glad Caroline wasn't able to come today."

Had Mary Warley known about this conversation she might have been less willing to arrange for the change of nurses. When the night nurse came in she, too, noticed a change in her patient.

Rosamund sat in an armchair while her bed was being arranged for the night. Jane and Raymond Quick, she was thinking: how would it be? Would Jane be dull and deferential, or lively and flirtatious? Should she tell Jane that Ray was her lawyer, her Lord Chamberlain, the one who held the power, the governor of her little world?

For the first time in many months Rosamund Morgan, the dying heiress, found herself positively looking forward to waking up in the morning.

"I think I'll listen to the concert," she said to the night nurse. "It's that new Spanish pianist playing late Beethoven sonatas. Could you put my radio back please, Mrs. Patterson?"

"Certainly, my dear."

"What are you going to do for the night?" asked Rosamund when she was settled in bed.

"Sit in the little room next door as usual. Read. Knit. Make tea. Write letters. Doze now and then."

"You don't get bored?"

"Not particularly. It's more or less what I'd be doing in the daytime."

"Nor lonely?"

"Well, of course one does feel a little isolated sometimes on night-work, but I'm used to it."

"You can always come and wake me up if you want a little chat."

"Oh no, Miss Morgan. I couldn't do that."

"I wouldn't mind. And I wish you would call me Rosamund. No, on second thoughts, I think perhaps I'd like a good night's sleep tonight. I want to be as fresh as possible tomorrow."

Tomorrow, thought the nurse; in all the weeks I've been coming here that's the first time I've heard her say a hopeful word about tomorrow. All the other nights she's gone to sleep with the look of someone who hopes never to wake again. So there has been a change. I thought it must come sometime or other. I wonder how long the remission will last, and what the rest of the household will make of it. Ah well, it's all the same to me, but some of them are going to be a bit put out.

Angela Patterson was the fifty-year-old widow of a well-known consultant psychiatrist. She was now working for the sake of having a purpose in life and not because she needed the money. She had many years of experience of nursing and was very interested in the interaction between mind and body. In her opinion patients could be divided into those who were determined to make a fight of it and those who did not want to live. From the very first she had classified Rosamund Morgan as one of the latter. She was too calm, too brave, too resigned. Outbursts of wild frustration or despair would have been more hopeful signs, clinically speaking. The puzzle was, why should so gifted and fortunate a creature as the Morgan heiress so willingly give up her hold on life? Was there some deep disappointment? An inherently depressive nature? Or was she oppressed by the burden of her own wealth, overwhelmed by the weight of expectation aroused in all those around her? It was as if she had taken on the role of dying heiress and was unable to get out of it.

Mrs. Patterson thought about Rosamund a great deal during her own solitary night-watching and wished there were somebody with whom she could discuss the case. She still talked a lot to her husband in her mind, although he had been dead for five years, but that was not good enough. She had never met Dr. Milton, and in any case one of these top consultant physicians was not the person she needed.

It was not that she was questioning the diagnosis. Obviously the bone marrow tests and the blood tests and the X-rays and all the rest of the frequent investigations were thorough and reliable. Rosamund definitely had a cancer of the blood that was rapidly getting worse and for which there was as yet no known cure. No physical cure, at any rate. But Angela Patterson had seen and experienced too much not to believe that miracles could happen. Only modern medicine didn't call them miracles: it called them spontaneous remissions.

What could have happened to turn Rosamund round into a more hopeful path? Angela never talked about her patient to Mrs. Warley or to the other nurses, or to anybody else whom she might come across during the course of her duties at Willoughby House. For this reason she was regarded as stand-offish and was not very popular, but Rosamund liked her, and Mr. Quick, who had met her briefly a couple of times, liked her too.

Mr. Quick, decided Angela Patterson after long reflection. He would be the one to talk to. Rosamund relied on him and trusted him without reservation. If, after a few more nights' observation, she came to the conclusion that there was some possibility of a recovery, however temporary, and that the gloomy weight of Rosamund's present surroundings was impeding it, then she would tell Mr. Quick her opinion. She felt sure that she would at least get a fair and sympathetic hearing.

3

"That was the nursing agency," said Jane putting down the receiver. "They want me at Willoughby House again tomorrow. And perhaps until further notice."

She did a little dance of joy around the crowded little room and ended by banging her knee against the sharp edge of the table leg.

"Ouch!" She collapsed onto Robert's lap, gasping, and grabbing at the sore spot.

"Shall I kiss it better?" he asked.

"No thanks. Cold water might be more help." She let go of her knee and flung her arms round his neck. "I'm so pleased. I was working away for her to ask me again."

"Jane." He held her at arms' length. "I'm glad you're happy but I'm also very suspicious. You wanted a rich patient and now you've got one. What's the big idea?"

"Nothing at the moment. Only to try and make her a little less unhappy. I actually made her laugh this afternoon. Shall I tell you?"

Robert could not pretend that he did not want to hear. Jane's account of her new patient had caught his imagination and sympathy to an almost painful degree. And he was only hearing it secondhand, whereas Jane had actually seen her. And although Jane might dream of great wealth and talk cheerfully about committing crimes to obtain it, she was no monster but a feeling human being and an exceptionally understanding nurse. Human motives were always mixed. It was unfair to attribute her interest in Rosamund Morgan purely to greed. And even before she had been to Willoughby House, Robert had had the impression that Jane was making a genuine effort to control her extravagant cravings. What could be more encouraging to such an effort than to meet a girl who possessed all that Jane longed for but who lacked the only thing that really mattered?

Surely Rosamund Morgan's influence on Jane must be for the good, financial benefit apart. Even the talking about her had drawn them closer together, wiping out the misery of yesterday evening's tension and bringing them harmony and comfort.

"Yes, tell me," said Robert. "How on earth did you manage to make her laugh? Slapstick stuff? Or scintillating wit?"

"Neither. I've no wit and I keep my slapstick for crashing into the furniture at home. I did it through you."

"Me? Where do I come in?"

He was as intrigued as she had intended. All was continuing to go very well.

"She was talking about not kicking against one's fate," said Jane, "and I told her I knew someone who never complained that he had had no chance in life, and she asked me more about you and said she'd like to meet you, and I said I didn't know whether it would be a good idea, and that upset her because she thought I meant you wouldn't want to see someone dying. So I said it wasn't that at all but that I was afraid you'd think her so wonderful that you'd be more discontented than ever with me."

Jane paused most effectively. She had returned to her own chair the better to observe the effect that her narration was having on him. He was trying hard to appear cool, sceptical, detached, but she knew that he was gripped.

"That's when she burst out laughing, at the idea of anyone being afraid she might steal their friend. So you see it wasn't really my doing at all—it was Rosamund laughing at herself. Don't you think that's wonderful?"

Robert felt disturbed by this story—puzzled, pleased, and vaguely apprehensive all at the same time. On the surface it all seemed very hopeful and encouraging, at any rate for Jane herself. The dying heiress teaches the discontented nurse a lesson in patience and resignation and then rewards her with a substantial legacy. A most attractive scenario. Was that what Jane was after?

Obviously she was angling for something, but she looked so glowing and so innocently pleased with herself that he was overwhelmed by his own need for her and revolted by his own suspicions.

"You will come and see Rosamund, won't you, darling?" she said later that night.

"Of course. If she really wants me to."

Mr. Quick drove his little Fiat along the few yards of unmade-up road and stopped alongside one of the white gateposts of Willoughby House. Only one of the high iron gates was open, but it was a sunny morning and he decided to leave the car outside and walk up the drive.

As he was strolling past the rhododendron bushes he heard the sound of men's voices and stopped to listen. Anything that happened at Willoughby House could affect

Rosamund. Eavesdropping was in a good cause. One of the voices was well-known to Mr. Quick.

"You told me to cut down that old lilac bush, and cut it down I have. And now you try telling me it was Miss Rosamund's favourite. I know what's the matter with you, Mr. Warley. She's getting better, ain't she? And you don't like that at all."

It was a slow, deliberate voice, mocking and very sure of itself. The fool, thought Mr. Quick, to think he can tangle with old George. Bill Warley's response was the predictable bluster.

"I suppose there's nothing more to be said," it concluded, "since the damage is done now. Just don't you do it again, that's all."

Mr. Quick walked on. He did not want to be caught listening and he had heard all he needed. So Bill Warley—which meant Mary too and Cousin John and anybody else who had expectations—was getting worried, was he? Rosamund better? Well, of course, she did have her up and down days, but it must have been something more dramatic than that to produce such an effect. The front door of Willoughby House was concealed behind a porch with a Gothic gable. Unattractive but useful in bad weather. Mr. Quick stared at its dingy yellow glazing as he rang the bell. Rosamund had given him a set of keys to the house, including those of her writing desk, but Mr. Quick would only use them in extreme emergency.

Mary Warley opened the door and they exchanged greetings. She appeared to be her usual calm and efficient self, but Mr. Quick, suspicions already aroused, read a different meaning into her words.

"You'll find a bit of a change in Rosamund. I don't quite know what to make of it."

"A change for the worse?"

They stood in the large square hall where the wall-lamps were always left burning because so little daylight came through.

"On the face of it, no," said Mary.

"You mean she's better?"

"On the face of it, yes. But I don't feel that we ought to be too hopeful," she went on hurriedly. "There's something unnatural, something almost hectic, about this sudden burst of energy. It could so easily precede an equally sudden relapse. I asked Dr. Milton to look in this afternoon. I felt it was advisable."

"I'm sure that was a very wise precaution," said Mr. Quick gravely. "Would it be convenient if I go and see Rosamund now?"

"She hasn't any other visitors this morning. I think the new nurse is with her at the moment."

Try as she would, Mary could not entirely keep the sharpness out of her voice as she spoke these last words. New nurse, thought Mr. Quick. Well, soon we shall see.

"Don't trouble to come with me," he said. "I believe I know my way by now."

She smiled in return, but it was clearly an effort. "I'll be in the breakfast room if anyone wants me," she said.

"Thanks," said Mr. Quick. "I'll look in before I go."

He turned to the right and walked along the short corridor at the end of which was the door of Rosamund's room. All this great house, all the great world outside, yet this one room was her only domain. And her prison. But perhaps no longer. Perhaps she would be able to sit in the garden again when the spring sunshine gained some strength; perhaps even a little drive over the Heath and a stop to look at the ducks on the pond. Such modest little joys swelled into great pleasures when one had not much time left in this world. Mr. Quick was unusually healthy for his eighty years, but there were many hours when he himself had the sense of an approaching end.

He knocked on the door and opened it upon a scene that drove away all thoughts of death. Rosamund, in her red dressing-gown and with a rug over her legs, was sitting in an armchair that had been drawn closer to the french windows. On a table by her side a few pieces of jigsaw puzzle had been fitted together. The divan bed was made up and the cover drawn right over it, and between Rosamund's chair and the bed there stood a small slim young woman in a white nurse's uniform pulling a starched cap off a mass of auburn curls and tossing her head as if released from an intolerable restraint.

Both she and Rosamund were laughing.

Mr. Quick stood just inside the door. This was a sound that he had never expected to hear again.

"Hullo, Ray." Rosamund turned her head. "You have to call him Mr. Quick," she said to Jane. "And none of your silly puns, please. He's heard quite enough of them."

"Will you introduce me," said the old man coming forward.

"Jane Bates." Rosamund waved a hand. "She says she's a nurse but I think she's a changeling. Or an apparition. Any minute now and she'll disappear in a cloud of smoke."

"Or on a broomstick," said Jane.

"A witch. Yes, that's right," said Rosamund. "She's cast a spell over me. I'm getting quite scared. Heaven knows what's going to happen next."

But she doesn't look scared, thought Mr. Quick; she looks relaxed and happy. Hectic and unnatural? Oh no, Mary Warley. It's these last months that have been unnatural, not today.

"Pleased to meet you, Jane Bates," he said holding out a hand.

She grasped it with surprising strength and said gravely: "I really am a State Registered Nurse, Mr. Quick. I can send you my references if you'd like to see them. Up till now I haven't done anything that might disgrace my profession."

"Except cheeking Matron," said Rosamund laughing again, and Jane joined her.

Like a couple of schoolgirls, thought Mr. Quick. Why hadn't anybody, not even Rosamund's own contemporaries, realized that this was the way to bring her to life? Perhaps they were too much in awe of her, of her money, her brains, her beauty, and her incurable illness. They all deferred to her, waited for her to call the tune, when all the time what she really needed was a little red-haired nurse who didn't seem to be in awe of anybody and who looked to possess vitality enough for two.

"Cheeking Matron? That's a very serious crime," said Mr. Quick taking the chair that Jane had placed for him.

"She got the sack for it," said Rosamund.

"I didn't," said Jane indignantly. "I resigned."

"Same thing." There was a mischievous look in Rosamund's eye.

Jane picked up a cushion from the divan and looked for a

moment as if she was about to start a fight, but she put it back instead and said: "No. Better wait till you're a bit stronger. But when that day comes—"

"'Just you wait, 'Enry 'Iggins, just you wait,'" quoted Rosamund.

Mr. Quick watched indulgently while they dissolved into giggles again.

When Jane had composed her face she said: "You'll be wanting to talk to Mr. Quick, Ros. Shall I make you coffee? Or does Mrs. Warley do it?"

Tactful too, thought Raymond Quick. And not above little domestic tasks, unlike some of the agency nurses who attended patients in luxury homes.

"That would be very kind," said Rosamund. "You'll find the things in the little room where you made tea yesterday afternoon."

Jane picked up her cap, pinned it into position, and left the room with a brisk and purposeful step.

"Well, well," said Mr. Quick after the door had closed behind her. "A witch indeed."

"What do you make of her?"

"She's certainly different," said Mr. Quick rather guardedly.

"You have reservations?"

"I always have. I'm stuffed tight with them. You know what a stuffy suspicious old creature I am."

"And I'm suspicious too. But I must say that if Jane Bates is trying to earn herself a little legacy, she's setting about it in a very unusual way."

"You're right there. Very different from that obsequious and obliging blonde girl."

"Poor Caroline. Will you send her a cheque for me, Ray? Whatever you think is appropriate. I don't think I shall be asking to have her back again."

"There is absolutely no need for you to give her anything at all."

"I know, but they all expect it, poor things. Except Mrs. Patterson. I would like to do something for her but I feel she'd rather I didn't. You must come along one evening and wait till she arrives and have a proper talk to her."

"I'd like that," said Mr. Quick.

They were silent for a moment, both looking out at the garden.

"What a lovely morning," said Rosamund. "The crocuses have all opened out to the sun."

"And the daffs are coming out and if this weather keeps up you'll soon be able to go outside a bit."

Mr. Quick turned to look at Rosamund as he spoke and saw the changing expression on her face. From being relaxed and peaceful it had suddenly become tense, almost frightened.

"That's what you were thinking, weren't you, my dear," he said very gently.

Rosamund was pressing against the arms of the chair, as if to lift herself up. She succeeded in half-rising and then fell back again as if suddenly overcome with weakness. She gave a little cry and then was silent except for the gasping breaths.

Raymond Quick, seriously alarmed, got up and came to her chair. She looked up at him and he saw that her eyes were brimming over with tears.

"Oh, Ray, oh, Ray!"

Her hands grabbed at his and clung to them.

"I'll call the nurse," he said. "Just let me go for a moment so that I can ring the bell."

"No, no. I'm not ill. It's just that—oh Ray! I can't bear it." And she leaned her face down on his hand and the thin frail body trembled and shook with sobs.

Mr. Quick, less alarmed now but still very much at a loss, murmured soothingly and stroked her hair. She's seen a vision of hope, he was saying to himself, and it's harder to endure than any amount of pain or despair. If only Jane Bates would come. It was she who had started this off; it was to be hoped that she would know how to deal with it because he certainly didn't know himself, and he was equally certainly not going to ask Mary Warley or Dr. Milton because they would say that the strain of sitting up had made Rosamund worse, and there would be fussing and sedatives and long faces and everything most calculated to drive that vision of hope away.

"Hurry up now, Nurse Bates," said Mr. Quick to himself out loud.

Rosamund continued to shake and sob. At last the door opened and Jane came in carrying a tray. Mr. Quick looked at her in mute appeal. Jane put down the tray on the table near the door and ran to Rosamund's side.

"I only said that it would be nice when she could go in the garden," said Mr. Quick. He gestured with his free hand as if to say, And look what it's done to her!

"Of course it'll be nice to go in the garden," said Jane in a matter-of-fact manner. "But it'll have to get quite a lot warmer first. Come on, Ros. Back into bed now. I've got a feeling that Mrs. Warley's going to turn up any minute and it won't do for her to find you weeping in a chair. She'll blame me and tell me I'm not to let you get up. She might even tell me not to come again."

"Oh, no." Rosamund's tears stopped as suddenly as they had begun and she allowed Jane to help her into bed.

"Is Mrs. Warley really on the way?" asked Mr. Quick when they were all three drinking their coffee.

"I don't know," said Jane, "but it worked, didn't it?"

Mr. Quick was looking at Rosamund. "Are you feeling better now?"

"Yes. I'm sorry. I don't know what came over me. Thank you—thank you both for not getting into a panic and sending for the doctor."

"Doctors!" exclaimed Jane. "I shouldn't take any notice of doctors if I were you. I never do myself."

"Nurse Bates," said Mr. Quick with mock severity. "I am very shocked to hear you talk like that. I had always understood that for members of your profession the doctor's word was law."

"Of course we have to pretend it is, but—why, what's the matter, Mr. Quick?" asked Jane as Mr. Quick interrupted with an exclamation of "Good heavens!"

"I nearly forgot," he went on. "Mrs. Warley told me that Dr. Milton is coming in this afternoon. I thought I'd better warn you."

"But it isn't his day," protested Rosamund.

"I thought so too, but that's what Mrs. Warley said."

"I wonder why." Looking rested and calm again now, Rosamund lay against the pillows and regarded Mr. Quick thoughtfully. "Did Mary send for him?" she asked at last.

"I believe so." Mr. Quick never found it easy to tell an outright lie.

"I see. Or rather, I think I see." Rosamund smiled. "All right. We'll be ready for him. Won't we, Jane?"

"If you don't feel confidence in him and would like to change your doctor," began Mr. Quick.

"Oh, I trust him all right. He's as good as any of them. He promised he wouldn't try to persuade me to any of the treatments that make your hair fall out and he's kept his word. But Jane will have to behave herself."

"Yes, Miss Morgan."

"And keep your cap on."

"Yes, Miss Morgan."

It was amazing, thought Mr. Quick, how rapidly Rosamund's storm of weeping had blown over. If it happened again he would try not to get too worried but to remember how the nurse had dealt with it. Just take it as a matter of course that Rosamund could be getting better. No denials, no warnings, no extravagant boosting of hopes. No emotional reaction. Of course it was easier for a trained nurse, and some of them seemed to have practised detachment so much that they had no feelings left at all, but he didn't think Jane Bates was like that. There was genuine human warmth in the joking and fooling about with Rosamund. That was sincere enough, even if only on the surface. What lay behind it Mr. Quick could not yet fathom. He only knew that the girl was very clever and very deep.

"Is it really necessary," Rosamund was saying, "for you girls to have a uniform cap?"

"No," replied Jane. "It's only because of the adverts. 'You can rely on North London Nurses for old-fashioned courtesy and care.'"

"But surely most of your work consists of supplying hospitals," said Mr. Quick. "Or it comes by doctors' recommendations. Do you really get any patients through newspaper advertisements?"

"Quite a few, I believe," replied Jane. "Lonely people with money to spare. They're not exactly ill so they don't want to see a doctor, but they're desperate for company so they get a nurse in mainly for a chat. Or they go to a beauty salon for the same reason."

"How terribly sad," said Rosamund. "How little one knows of other people's lives."

"Yes, I think I can understand it," said Mr. Quick. "I used to have a number of clients like that during my working years."

When Mary Warley came into the room a moment later she sensed at once that she was interrupting a conversation that was absorbing all three of them.

". . . you don't mean that it's young people too," Rosamund was saying. She broke off when she saw her cousin come forward into the room. "Hullo, Mary. Are you going to join us for coffee?"

"No thanks. I've had mine."

She glanced from one to the other of them. Mr. Quick had risen and was standing by his chair. Nurse Bates was replacing the coffee cups on the tray. Rosamund was lying in bed in her usual position. Everything looked exactly as it had looked the previous day and for many weeks past. Yet Mary felt a difference. There was something in the air. Hostility? Conspiracy? Whatever it was, she herself was excluded. Subtly, indefinably, but very surely, it was being conveyed to her that she herself was no longer in control of what went on in this room. But which of the three was responsible? How and where could she fight back?

"Have I interrupted a business conference?" She turned to Mr. Quick. "It isn't important. I can come back later."

"Not at all," he replied. "We've no business to discuss today. We were actually talking about the problem of loneliness in modern society."

"Oh, yes." Mary rapidly adjusted her thoughts. "Did you watch that television programme last Sunday?"

"Some of it," replied Mr. Quick.

Jane finished arranging the tray, picked it up, and carried it out of the room.

"What do you think of her?" said Mary to Mr. Quick when the door had closed again.

"She seems cheerful and efficient," he replied.

"You don't think—" She stopped. She wanted to say, you don't think she's having a disturbing effect on Rosamund, but one could hardly say that in Rosamund's presence, and in any case the girl herself looked so peaceful and undisturbed that Mary realized it would sound absurd.

"I like her," said Rosamund placidly. "She amuses me."

She sounded exactly as she had on the previous evening when Mary, at that time still without suspicion, had agreed to ask the agency for Nurse Bates again. If only she had refused! Or had pretended to ask and then told Rosamund that Nurse Bates was not available. But it was too late now for such simple solutions. Mr. Quick would see to that.

Mr. Raymond Quick, whose word was law, who guided all Rosamund's decisions, who held all Mary's and everybody else's expectations in his hands. On no account must one offend Mr. Quick nor arouse his suspicions. Even Mary Warley was not, in the last resort, indispensable. And if she lost her position in this house . . . Well, of course it was unthinkable that her services would go unrewarded, and apart from John Aylmer, she was Rosamund's nearest relative, but nevertheless, one never knew.

Once again Mary was seized by the thought that had so shattered her the previous evening. Why, oh why, couldn't Rosamund die now, quickly and painlessly, when everyone about her had done their duty and the money was suitably disposed of? It had to happen soon, so why prolong the agony? And it was so easy. Rosamund's illness took away every bit of resistance to minor infections. Even a slight chill, or stomach upset, or too many pain-killers or sedatives.

It would take so little to tip her over. Perhaps Dr. Milton . . . No, of course not Dr. Milton. Mary succeeded in getting a grip on her racing thoughts. She would have to go very very carefully. Particularly with Dr. Milton and with the three people in this room. Tackle them one at a time. The nurse was the easiest. Perhaps she might arrange to do more for Rosamund herself. All this nursing was not really necessary, as Rosamund had remarked. It was simply in line with the overall running of the establishment. Mary liked spending money, and in this case there was no danger of depleting the estate.

But she had nursing experience herself, and she had taken care of Rosamund before the last spell in hospital. She could perfectly well cope with a lot more than she did now. What excuse to give? That would take some thought.

"That's fine then," she said to Rosamund, "if Nurse Bates amuses you. I can see for myself that she's done you good."

"She has indeed, and I want her to bring her friend soon. I must not forget to ask her about it this afternoon."

"Oh, yes. That's what I came in for," said Mary. "This afternoon. Dr. Milton will be looking in about tea-time."

"Yes, I know. Mr. Quick told me."

"Mr. Quick?" Mary had momentarily forgotten her own brief exchange with Mr. Quick when he arrived at the house. The little lapse of memory frightened her even further. It was unlike her to slip up like this. But then she was not naturally secretive. Her incapacity for scheming did not fit well with her longing to resolve the situation to her own advantage. She felt more and more confused and took refuge on familiar ground.

"Would you like to stay to lunch, Mr. Quick? It'll be just you and my husband and myself. Caroline used to join us sometimes, but I expect Rosamund would like her new nurse to sit and eat with her."

Rosamund agreed. Mr. Quick expressed his thanks but declined on this occasion. Perhaps another time. Mary Warley left the room with everything restored to normal, at least on the surface. Mr. Quick said goodbye to Rosamund, promising to come next day, and she promised him that she would now rest a little.

Outside the room he paused a moment. It was not necessary to see Mrs. Warley again but he felt an urgent need to talk to the nurse. If it had been anybody but Jane he would have known exactly what to say, or rather what to hint: take good care of Miss Morgan and it will be made worth your while. But Jane was not like the others. It was impossible even to guess at what was going on in her mind. On the one hand she might be a most valuable assistant spy in the house, reporting to Mr. Quick if anyone had worried Rosamund in any way. But on the other hand she herself might well be the chief instigator of the worry.

Perhaps it was wisest to say nothing just yet but simply wait and watch, and meanwhile take Jane at her face value —which meant gratefully to accept the fact that she radiated vitality, and that some of it had spilled over onto Rosamund.

He found her in the little room that was put aside for the nurses, equipped as part sitting-room, part pantry, and part surgery. The coffee cups were washed and standing on the table beside the sink, and she was rearranging the bottles of medicines and packets of tablets in the wall cabinet.

"Miss Bates?"

"Yes, Mr. Quick?"

She turned round, bright, friendly, and courteous: everything that Rosamund's nurse ought to be.

"I want to thank you for what you are doing for Miss Morgan. You must understand that she is like a daughter—or rather, like a granddaughter to me. To ensure that she has as much comfort and as little suffering as possible is the chief aim of my life."

"I can quite understand that, sir."

It was spoken sincerely, respectfully, without the slightest hint of mockery.

"If ever you feel you would like to speak to me about her," he went on, "here is my card. As you see, I do not live very far away. I can be here any time, with about twenty minutes' notice. There's just one more thing I'd like to say."

Jane waited expectantly.

"I have been obliged in watching over Miss Morgan to learn something of the nature of this terrible illness and I cannot deceive myself into hoping for any permanent cure. Five years from the onset of the disease is, I believe, the most that can be expected. She has been ill for about three and a half years and in recent months seems to have deteriorated rapidly. Do you think, Miss Bates, that what we are seeing at the moment is a one-day flash in the pan, or a one-week or one-month? Or do you think there is any possibility that she might return to, say, another year or even more of a somewhat more active and worthwhile kind of life?"

Jane was listening intently. When he had finished she said, "I feel flattered by your asking me. I've never nursed a leukaemia patient before, except a little boy in hospital who died the week after I started the job. I honestly don't know what to say. It depends so much on the patient. One of my teachers used to say that cancer was a socially acceptable form of suicide. Maybe that's going rather far, but there's no doubt that people do seem to succumb to it and get rapidly worse when they have lost the will to live."

"You think Miss Morgan has lost the will to live?"

"Yes. Don't you?"

Mr. Quick responded with another question: "Do you think that outburst of hers this morning was a healthy sign?"

"It could be. We shall have to wait and see. I want her to meet my friend. He could do a lot for her. He's a rather wonderful person in his way. May I introduce him to you too?"

Mr. Quick could do no other than say yes. He asked her a few questions about herself and about her friend, receiving what seemed to be perfectly satisfactory answers, and he went away at last as baffled by Jane as before, admiring her, fascinated by her, but still not knowing whether to be hopeful or apprehensive about her influence on Rosamund's life.

4

"When's your free afternoon this week?" asked Jane.

"Friday," called out Robert from the kitchen. He had offered to cook the meal again and also to do the shopping. So far Jane had made no comment on the very obvious smell of boiling chicken. It was not expensive and with herbs and extras could be very tasty. Harmony still reigned in their modest home.

"Why?" he added. "Have you got the day off?"

"Tell you later. That smells good. Hurry it up, darling. I'm hungry."

"Don't they feed you in your millionaire's mansion?"

"And how! Smoked salmon, avocado salads. Lovely grub. But I eat with Rosamund and she only picks at it, poor soul. Which makes it awfully difficult for me to guzzle."

Robert's reply was lost in the hiss of chopped vegetables being dropped into very hot fat.

"I'm changing my clothes," called Jane through the open door of the bedroom. "We're not going out this evening, are we?"

"Not that I know of."

A few minutes later she was asking where he had put the evening paper. This was usually a dangerous moment. Jane would turn straight to the estate agents' advertisements and begin to dream aloud. But this evening that too was changed, and she read him out titbits of news while he took the bones out of the chicken and set the rice to cook. She even forgot their sherry and he decided not to remind her.

"How's college?" she asked as they sat down to eat.

"Much as usual." Then, since she did not as he had expected go on to an account of her own day's activities, he added: "I've got a new student. Wants a crash course for the English A level. An American. His father's taken an academic post in England for a few years. Bright boy. He might just make it in the time. And it makes a change from the Iranians and the Nigerians, poor devils. They're all right in the science and technology courses but it seems so daft to expect them to make sense out of nineteenth-century English novels."

"What's the matter with Victorian novels?"

Jane sounded a little indignant. She herself loved to read the great Victorian writers, and Robert sometimes wondered whether this was perhaps the source of her notions of how to live the good life.

"Nothing the matter at all," he replied, "provided you've got the sort of cultural background to appreciate them."

"Oh, I see. But why should an American boy be any better than any of the other overseas students?"

"Because it is the same cultural background. And anyway his favourite author is Henry James, and you couldn't get more Anglo-American, or European-American, than that."

"Henry James," repeated Jane thoughtfully. "I read about half a dozen of them straight off a couple of years ago. Do you remember? I think I'll go back to him when I've finished my stretch of Trollope."

"In that case I might come to you for help," said Robert.

"I've always found him tough going and tried to avoid him. But I'll have to struggle through some of the novels myself. I believe I'll actually have to be teaching one as a set book."

"Which one?"

"Can't remember. Was it *Washington Square?* No, I don't think so. I'll let you know when I find out. If you're really interested, that is."

For Jane to ask such detailed questions about Robert's work was not entirely unknown, but it was unusual enough to cause him a certain amount of puzzlement. A few days ago he might have suspected that it was only a prelude to one of her periodic onslaughts on him to make a more profitable use of his talents than his present teaching job, but tonight he was tempted to attribute it to what was beginning to look more and more like some sort of permanent change in Jane's attitude. In other words, to the influence of Rosamund Morgan, and it was high time that Jane reported on her own day's events.

"What's this about Friday afternoon?" he asked.

"If you're free you could come and see Rosamund."

"If you're sure she really wants—"

"She's longing to meet you. She plays chess, by the way. I don't suppose she's up to your standard, but perhaps you wouldn't mind descending from the heights for once."

Thus it was arranged. Almost too easy, thought Jane. But she would have to be careful about Robert. This last conversation with him had made her very wary. There was a distinct danger that he might come to suspect and to revolt and ruin the whole thing before he was too deeply involved to draw back. He was her main worry. Or rather, that part of him that she knew so little about and that had burst through in that frightening way when she had pushed him too far.

The hostility towards her at Willoughby House she could take in her stride. It was a matter of playing the correct role with the Warleys and Dr. Milton and George the gardener and Mrs. Miller the daily cleaner, and anyone else whom she chanced to meet; a rather different role with the all-important Mr. Quick; and just being herself with Rosamund. That was the great beauty of the whole plan, that she didn't have to put on an act with Rosamund, that she was in no way betraying Rosamund nor adding to the sick girl's burdens.

Rather the contrary. She was doing Rosamund good. Everybody could see that. Hence the panic. But Jane's own conscience towards Rosamund was absolutely clear. She was brightening Rosamund's days and she would continue to do so, right up to the very end, if she was allowed to. And the fact that Rosamund was such a lovely person, whom one could truly admire and love—well that was what made it all possible and so very worthwhile.

So simple, so neat, and so subtle. Again and again Jane found herself marvelling at the plan. Was this how Robert felt when he went into ecstasies over his chess problems? What a pity they could not share the anticipation and the joy. Perhaps later? No, never. Eventually there was going to come a very bad moment with Robert, and the more successful the scheme, the worse the moment. It was best not to worry about it till it came. She would cope with it somehow.

On Friday morning she gave him detailed instructions about how to get to Willoughby House, told him to arrive at three-thirty and to tell whoever opened the door, which would probably be one of the Warleys but might be Mrs. Miller, that Miss Morgan had invited him to visit her at this hour.

"Don't mention me," Jane added. "Just give your name and say that Miss Morgan has invited you. Rosamund has told them to expect you, but they may fuss a bit and say they'd better make sure she's well enough to receive visitors. They will fuss so over her and she hates it. O.K., darling?"

"I suppose so," said Robert rather uneasily.

She kissed him goodbye, went to the front door, and then turned and said as if it were an afterthought: "Oh, by the way, I've never actually told Rosamund that we live together. Obviously she realizes that we do, but I don't actually talk about it."

"You mean she'd disapprove?" Robert was puzzled as well as increasingly uneasy.

Jane laughed. "Of course not. She's twenty-five, not fifty-two. I'm sure Mr. Quick realizes it too, and he's eighty and he doesn't disapprove. It's nothing to do with morals, it's more a matter of taste. You see when someone's as ill as Rosamund—and even though she's brightened up a bit she's still terribly ill and there isn't the slightest chance that she'll ever recover—then you have to be careful what you talk about. She never complains about being cut off from life and she tries hard to take an interest in other people's activities but it's not easy. You can see it's a strain on her when her college friends talk about their love affairs and their future prospects. Get me, darling?"

"You mean because she hasn't any herself? Yes, I see. All right. I'll do my best."

"I knew you'd understand." She kissed him again and ran off down the road. Robert's pupils found him rather absent-minded that morning, which was unusual. At a quarter to three he was walking across Hampstead Heath, killing time until the moment came to arrive at Willoughby House, and at exactly twenty-five minutes past three he stood by the white gateposts, looking up the drive towards the front entrance. He felt as if he were going to execution, not on a social visit.

The size and the scale of the place made him more nervous than ever. What right had he to visit at this grand house? He, a nobody in every sense of the word, socially of no consequence, legally without a name. He wasn't even here on business, like Jane or like the driver of that delivery van just now turning into the tradesmen's entrance a little further along the lane. It was like one of Jane's favourite Victorian novels, and she had managed to scramble inside it, but he was the outcast, the outsider.

Underneath all the surface anxiety, Robert began to be aware of the stirring of a much deeper pain. It was as if a numbness was wearing off, a numbness that had been part of him for a very long time. But it was not the glorious coming to life that Jane in their early days had brought to him. It was more like being dragged out of a merciful anaesthetic, and every step he took strengthened the conscious apprehension and the deep inner sense of foreboding.

He knew this place. He had been here before. The wide sweep of gravel, the high dark shrubs on either side. The size and strangeness of it all. The fear of it. Because all of consciousness was fear and pain. Only he didn't know it, because like a wounded animal he felt but knew nothing, until suddenly he was in this place where he knew himself and felt how sharp had been the pain.

The adult Robert heard the sound of a car and fought to

free himself from the memories that were drowning him. He looked back towards the entrance and saw a man bending down to fix the gate-stop. With a great wrench of thought he pulled himself back into the present. This was the house where Jane—who was Jane? Yes, of course he knew Jane. This was where Jane was nursing a rich patient, a girl dying of leukaemia, who for some reasons or other had expressed a wish to meet him. And the identity that he was fighting so hard to regain was that of Robert Fenniman, aged twenty-nine, a teacher of English, a taxpayer, a responsible and law-abiding citizen of British nationality.

Except that he didn't know even that. He was white-skinned, that was undeniable, but for all he knew his mother might have been Dutch or Swedish or American or a girl from some Catholic country who had come to England to take advantage of the easier abortion laws but failed to carry through her intentions.

The man at the gate was straightening up. Robert turned round again and hurried on up the drive. There was no doubt that that man knew exactly who and where he was. He had fixed the gates with the air of a proprietor and Robert had caught a glimpse of the Alfa Romeo. His instinct was to turn and run away. He did not know how he was going to get through this visit at all, how he was going to keep the mask of his adult self afloat above the tide of memory, and if he was not to be the only visitor it would be even worse. But to run away meant facing the man who was now driving in at the front entrance, and at this moment Robert was incapable of facing anybody.

Not because he was afraid that they might see him and despise and reject him, but because he was afraid they might not see him at all.

Robert reached the front door and rang the bell. He heard the sound of tyres crunching on the gravel but he did not turn round. He stared at the ugly yellow glass and prayed: let them come quick, this second, just so that I get in first.

A closed door. And he was locked out in the street. Another memory? At any rate, it felt only too familiar. Please let the door be opened now. Please let him enter this house in the character of the man he had taught himself to be. And please let this man be recognized and greeted by another so that this awful drowning pain of nothingness would come to an end.

"Have you rung?" asked a voice just behind him.

Robert turned to see a man of about his own age and height, dark-eyed, dark-haired, good-looking in an oddly old-fashioned manner—a sort of nineteen-thirties film star.

"Yes, I've just rung," he replied.

The other said no more and for a few moments they stood side by side. Robert looked at the glass in the door. He could feel the other staring at him and appraising him. It was not a friendly stare. Robert could sense the enmity and contempt. But at least it implied a sort of recognition. It was better than being completely overlooked and ignored.

The door was opened at last. A grey-haired red-faced man of stocky build glanced at Robert indifferently and then smiled and stretched out a hand to the other.

"Hullo, John. Good to see you."

"Hi to you, Bill. Mary all right?"

"Busy. Busy as usual. But she'll be glad to see you."

"And Rosie?"

The smile disappeared and the red face assumed an undertaker's gravity. "Worrying. Very worrying. Mary wants to see you about it. Looks as if something is going to have to be done."

He opened the door wide and the other man walked through. The door would then have been closed again if Robert had not stepped forward and put his foot in the way.

Like a door-to-door salesman, he thought grimly. The fear and the apprehension and the terrible sense of having no substance or reality at all were still very much with him, but so was something else. A very different sort of feeling that warmed and strengthened and brought him to life. It was anger. Not the impotent rage of the battered child but the fury of the adult who knew his own strength.

"Just a minute," said Robert.

"Oh," said the red-faced man feebly. "Did you want something?"

A frightened bully, thought Robert; I could knock him out in a second. This knowledge enabled him to speak with polite determination.

"Miss Morgan is expecting me. My name is Robert Fenniman. She suggested that I should come at three-thirty and I believe it's just that now."

"Oh," said the red-faced man again, looking rather taken aback. "I don't know whether it will be possible for you to see Miss Morgan just now. She's very much an invalid, as I expect you know, and that was her cousin who's just gone in, so she won't be free this afternoon."

Bill Warley paused. Robert neither moved nor spoke. He was holding on to his anger as to a lifeline.

Bill cleared his throat. "If you want anything from Miss

Morgan it would be best to write. Or better still, get in touch with her lawyer who handles all her charitable donations. I can give you his address."

This speech of Bill's, which was intended to insult and offend, had in fact the opposite effect. It strengthened Robert's failing will and gave him the power to reply.

"I am not interested in charitable donations. I am begging neither for myself nor for anybody else. I have come on a purely social visit to Miss Morgan at her own request. Will you be good enough to let her know that I am here?"

There was a moment's silence while Bill Warley took stock of the visitor and wished he had kept John Aylmer by his side. They ought to have handled this together. John would have known what to do. Bill felt a sudden surge of anger against John. Why had he gone on ahead? He ought to have stayed to help. After all, John would be the main loser if some man spun a hard-luck story to Rosamund and wheedled money out of her. It was just like John to leave Bill to do the dirty work. The whole house had been alive with gossip about the new nurse and her "friend" whom Ros was so anxious to meet. But somehow or other they had not expected anybody quite like this. They had pictured him as some insidious little creep who could be bought off with bribes if not driven away by threats.

Bill hadn't expected this formidable-looking fellow, half his age and twice his strength. A strange-looking face. Pale blue eyes, high cheekbones, a wide firm mouth. Almost Slav-looking. Spoke quite normally though. No sort of an accent. But that didn't mean anything. Any con man worth his salt would know how to put on the right act.

So what was he going to do now? They couldn't stand

here for ever, and nobody else looked like coming to the rescue.

"All right," he said very ungraciously. "I'll tell her. Wait here." He glanced around as if wondering whether it was safe to leave the visitor alone in the porch with the house door open. He had not the slightest idea that Robert's determination was fast ebbing away and that he was very near to the end of his strength.

After Bill had gone Robert leaned against the wall of the porch and shut his eyes. Lines from *Henry V* came into his head: "Once more unto the breach . . ."

He did indeed feel as if he was fighting a battle against impossible odds, but the enemy was not Bill Warley, nor the snooty cousin, nor all the ambiance of this great house. The enemy lay deep within himself. It was a small, hopeless and helpless child who knew nothing except how to grasp for the food and try to ignore the blows. That child had now taken him over completely. If Bill Warley had stood firm and said, "I'm sorry, but you can't see Miss Morgan just now," Robert the adult would have turned and walked away.

He knew this, and he tried to use this short breathing space to conquer the child and to dredge up some more strength of will.

It was useless. The conviction of his own nothingness filled all consciousness. It was all he could do to remain where he was.

After a long time he heard a woman's voice.

"Mr. Fenniman? I'm sorry you've been kept waiting."

A cold voice. Formal and polite. There was once a social worker, a child care officer, who had had much the same sort of voice. Perhaps it was the one who had come to take him away from the face with the dark eyes that really looked at him and the voice that had spoken his name.

At any rate, this grey-haired woman's voice seemed to blend into the whirlpool of past and present that was engulfing his consciousness.

"Miss Morgan is expecting you," it went on. "I'm afraid my husband had not been told, but he came to the door when he heard Mr. Aylmer's car and naturally did not expect to see anybody else. I'm sure you will understand that someone in Miss Morgan's position has to be protected. People can be very obtrusive and thoughtless sometimes."

Robert managed to speak. "I quite understand."

It seemed that the battle had been won. The struggle to get into the house was behind him, and yet again he had survived. But the cost had been too high. He had lost his survival kit, and the protective shell that alone enabled him to keep up some appearance of self-assurance seemed to be dissolving along with everything else.

"Come this way," said Mary Warley, and Robert moved after her like a zombie.

She pushed open a door. "Here's Mr. Fenniman, dear. He quite understands that you're not up to a long visit."

Robert walked into the room. He was conscious of brightness and space; of sunshine and green grass in the distance; of bookshelves and a television screen and yellow armchairs and a stretch of light-coloured carpet. The whole room seemed to be swimming in light. He felt weak and giddy. Everything was moving and swaying around him.

And then he heard the voice.

"Robert Fenniman," it said. "How lovely to meet you."

The voice! He moved forward. He heard somebody say the words, "Thank you for inviting me, Miss Morgan," but he did not know who it was.

The voice spoke again. "I'm afraid I'm going to have to ask you to go now, John."

Robert gripped the back of a chair to try to steady himself. He had not yet looked at the owner of the voice, but he became conscious that there was a third person in the room.

"I'm sorry, John," went on Rosamund, "but you ought to have let me know you were thinking of coming. I could have told you I wouldn't be free and have saved you a journey."

John Aylmer got up from one of the yellow armchairs. Robert did not see the glance of pure hatred that he gave him. He was staring out of the window at the lawn and the beech tree and the crocuses. Memory had converted them into an overgrown orchard, a strange and exciting world to explore. He had no idea where that large house had been where he had spent that happy time, but certainly the approach and the front entrance must have been rather similar to that of Willoughby House.

A man's voice was speaking. It did not belong to the memory and Robert could not understand why it was there.

"I suppose I shall have to leave you," it said. "But I give you up with a very bad grace, my dear sweet coz. However, I can pop in and see you any time." John Aylmer bent to kiss Rosamund. "I can see you are about to add yet another to your long list of conquests. Don't be too hard on the poor man."

Robert continued to cling to the back of the chair and to gaze out of the window. The man's words had reached his ears but his mind had given them no meaning. He heard the sound of a door closing but still he could not move. Then the voice spoke again.

"Won't you come nearer, Robert? I can hardly see you there."

He moved his head in the direction of the voice. Rosamund was lying on the divan in her red dressing-gown with the rug covering her feet. Her head was turned towards him and she was holding out a hand and smiling at him.

Robert let go of the chair at last and walked forward as if hypnotized.

"That's better," said Rosamund. "Pull up a chair."

Robert reached out vaguely behind him. He could not keep his eyes from Rosamund's face. The fear that he might lose it again was beyond endurance. He stared and stared as if to fix it for ever and ever.

Rosamund began to look slightly puzzled and slightly anxious. She said something, but this time Robert did not hear. Without knowing in the least what he was doing he moved forward and knelt down by the side of the divan and took hold of Rosamund's hand. A voice from his adult self cried, You're mad! Take a grip on yourself!

He tried to heed it but failed. He looked up at Rosamund's face and saw the dark eyes grow dim from the moisture in his own. He shook his head in a last attempt to ward off the storm but it was much too late. The last fragments of his shell had melted away for ever and all he could do was lay his burning cheek against the coolness of her thin fingers and wish that he was dead.

"It's all right, Robert," she said. "It'll go over in a minute or two. I did this myself the other day. Suddenly, quite out of the blue. I know just what it feels like."

Presently she said: "Better now? Then bring up that chair and we'll arrange ourselves into an appropriate tableau. People are supposed to knock before coming in but one can never be sure. That's the worst of being an invalid. You are deprived of the luxury of privacy."

5

"Jane didn't exaggerate," said Robert. "She said you were more beautiful than anybody she had ever seen."

He was sitting, dry-eyed and comparatively calm, a few feet away from where Rosamund lay.

"Does she normally exaggerate?" asked Rosamund.

"She does sometimes," he replied, wondering why he had felt obliged to mention Jane straight away. Was it because he felt a vague sense of disloyalty towards her? She was the brightness and the anchor of his life and yet in all their years together he had never behaved as he had just now done with Rosamund, meeting her for the very first time. But then Jane wouldn't have wanted him to. She didn't like weakness.

"Where is she?" he added. "I thought I'd find her here with you."

"She has been tactfully busying herself in the nurses' room. And now she is tactfully leaving us alone. Unless you want to see her?"

Robert shook his head. "Later on. I just wondered whether she was here."

"She'll bring us some tea presently. Let me look at you properly. That's better. No, I don't think she exaggerated about you either."

"Not perfectly beautiful?"

They both laughed.

"Not that," said Rosamund. "Something rather more valuable perhaps. I'll tell you some time. When we've got to know each other a little better."

"So I'm to come again?"

"Only if you'd like to. Would you like to? Can you spare the time?"

Her voice sounded suddenly unsure, even slightly pitiful. Robert felt moved almost beyond endurance.

"I'd love to come," he said, "but your cousin—"

"Oh Robert, I'm so very sorry you had such a horrible reception. It was very brave of you to come at all and it was most unfortunate that John should turn up at the same time. I told my other cousin, Mrs. Warley, who keeps house for me, that you'd be coming at about half-past three but I don't think she can have passed on the message to her husband. It's most unusual for him to answer the bell. I'm most deeply sorry about it. They feel they have to protect me, you see, and sometimes they get a bit over-zealous."

She's working very hard at excusing them, thought Robert. It was what he would do himself in the circumstances. Jane had said that he and Rosamund had similarities in character. It seemed an odd thing to say, but he was beginning to see what she meant.

"Try not to worry about John," Rosamund went on. "He thinks he's got to be very possessive about me, being my nearest relative, but he'll just have to put up with it. I'm afraid that if you run into him again you can hardly expect him to be friendly, but he'll never go too far. He's got too much to lose. So if you could bear with them, Robert, I'd be enormously grateful."

It was as if he was doing her the favour, not the other way round. He stammered out something about being rather overwhelmed and then added more firmly that he didn't want to tire her with talking.

"I'll tell you when I'm tired," she said, "and you must tell me if you are bored with being here."

"Bored!"

"Yes. Don't look so horrified. Visiting an invalid can be very boring. But we won't talk about that any more," she hurried on. "Don't let's waste any more time talking about unimportant things. I want to hear about yourself. I'm wondering what came over you just now after John left us alone. Or would you rather not tell me?"

"I'd like to tell you. It might help me to understand it better myself. Did Jane ever tell you that I was a foundling and that I don't know who my parents were and never will know?"

"She told me," replied Rosamund, "but I find it very difficult to understand what that must feel like. However, I will try my best."

"And I can't understand what it must feel like to be otherwise. It makes me smile when students talk about their problem of identity."

They smiled at each other.

"That's what caused it, I think," said Robert. "You see, I was brought up in a series of foster homes, and while only one of them was outstandingly bad, most of them were concerned purely with rearing a tolerably healthy young animal but not a conscious and questioning human being."

"And what about the outstandingly bad one?"

"I was about six years old, I suppose. There was a public scandal about it. Indignant letters to the papers. You know the sort of thing. If you don't mind, I'd rather not talk about that at the moment, because it's what followed that mattered so much. I was taken to a sort of battered babies refuge, in a house not unlike this one, and as I walked up the drive just now the memories came flooding over me."

He paused and looked out of the window again, but Rosamund noted the change of expression. She waited silently.

"I don't know how long I was there," he went on. "A month seems like a year when you are that age. But it was the most important part of my whole life. Not just because it was kind and safe and happy, but for a very particular reason. There was a girl there. She must have been one of the helpers. It was some sort of church group. She must have taken a special interest in me. I suppose I was her special job and she did it very well."

He was still staring out of the window and he did not see Rosamund's features contract when he spoke the last words.

"Before then I don't think I'd even known who I was. I mean that I had no consciousness of being an individual human being. I think I must have come when called and done what I was told to do rather as if I was a dog. But when this girl spoke to me it was as if I realized for the first time that I was really me." He turned to her and smiled. "Perhaps I am making too much of the whole business. I suppose there is a moment in every child's life when it first becomes conscious of its identity."

"Yes, in a sense I suppose there is." Rosamund was still frowning. "But not quite in the way I think you mean. I don't think you are making too much of it at all. I think something overwhelmingly important must have happened to you at that time."

"It certainly felt like it. It felt like being brought to life."

"And what came after?"

"I was taken away again. It wasn't a permanent children's home. Only an emergency place."

"And the girl?" asked Rosamund faintly.

"Oh. I never saw her any more." Robert replied in the most matter-of-fact manner. "She was one of the staff. I don't know what she was called."

Rosamund made no reply. Robert glanced at her and the next moment he was once again kneeling by her side.

"Rosamund, dear Rosamund. Don't cry. There's no need to cry. I didn't tell you this to make you weep. I only wanted to explain. You see I sort of remembered her face. It was like your own. And so was her voice. And that's why I went and collapsed on you just now. It was just the memory. And now it's gone and I shan't see and hear her any more. It's all melted away into you."

He had hold of her hands again. "I want to thank you for giving life to the best of my memories. I must have been looking for her ever since that time and now I don't have to search any more."

"I think, I think—" Rosamund withdrew one hand and passed it over his hair—"I think we had better talk about something else now," she continued more firmly.

"Of course." Robert got up and returned to his chair. "There's no need to say any more about it. I knew you'd understand."

"I understand." Rosamund nodded. "Oh yes. I understand." She leaned back against the pillows and closed her eyes. Robert sat quiet and still, looking at her very tenderly. There was no need to ask whether she was tired and wished him to go away. He knew that she wanted him to stay and that presently she would say something more. I have found her, he said to himself, and she is exactly what I believed her to be. He was conscious of a great sense of peace as if his journeyings were now at an end, and the words formed in his mind: "I have come home."

For several minutes they remained thus in silence. Then Rosamund opened her eyes and said: "Well! Shall we leave the past aside for a while and come back to the present? You're teaching foreign students, aren't you?"

He told her a little about his job. "I like it," he added a little defensively as if he were arguing with Jane. "It's looked down on by the academics, but I'd never do as a university teacher. I couldn't cope with all the infighting."

"I don't blame you. How about the chess?"

"Ah. That's my escape."

She produced a book of problems that she had been studying. "Do you know this one?"

Robert pulled his chair nearer and they bent over it together. "No, I don't think so," he said.

"I've been trying it, but the least I can get down to is seven moves."

"May I take it?"

"Please. And next time you come perhaps you'll explain it to me."

"And perhaps I can ask you some questions about yourself instead of doing all the talking."

He saw that she was now beginning to tire. She leaned back again and closed her eyes for a moment and seemed to be very far away.

"If you really want me to," she said at last, "I'll talk some more about myself. Could you touch that bell there? Thanks. I told Jane I'd ring."

He pushed his chair back and was standing at the window looking out at the lawn with the crocuses when the door opened.

"I've been hearing Robert's life history," said Rosamund rousing herself and smiling at Jane. "We've stopped now for tea-break."

"It's all ready. I'll fetch it. Hullo, Robert."

He turned round. "Hi there, Jane. You've got yourself a super job this time."

"Haven't I? Rosamund's my favourite patient ever."

There was a slight awkwardness. Even Jane could not quite hide it. After she had gone, and Robert was arranging the table and chairs according to Rosamund's instructions, he found himself wondering what Jane would think if she knew how his first meeting with Rosamund had begun. Should he try to tell her? No, because it would mean explaining so much and he did not know how he would be able to make it clear to Jane. He would have to start off with recounting that memory, which now seemed so unimportant because it had become submerged in Rosamund; and then he would somehow have to try to explain why he had known that Rosamund would understand but had never felt that Jane would really understand, and that would be almost like saying that he preferred Rosamund to Jane, which was absurd.

Far better to say nothing. After all, it would not happen again. On future visits to Rosamund they would just talk about things that interested them both. And when Jane asked him what he thought of her, he would simply say how wonderful and brave she was, but would not mention his own collapse and Rosamund's healing touch and voice.

By the time Jane returned with the tea-tray his doubts

had been resolved and the slight sense of strain had gone and the three of them were happy together.

"Next time you come I shall be sitting up in a chair," said Rosamund. "I was up yesterday and the day before but Jane thought I'd better stay in bed today and not try to rush things. She was right as usual."

The girls smiled at each other and Robert was filled with a warm sense of comfort. It was all right. They understood each other perfectly. There was no need to feel that he need tell Jane everything that Rosamund said to him or he to her. After all, it was Jane herself who had arranged this meeting and who had made a joke about being afraid she might have cause to feel jealous of Rosamund. They would very likely remember it and laugh about it after he had gone.

It was all right. He and Jane would do their best to give Rosamund some happy hours. It would be a fresh bond between them. And as for the cousin—well, as Rosamund said, that was her own business. The best thing that Robert could do was to keep out of his way, and if ever he got a chance to make the cousins understand that he was no threat to them, he would take it. To be firm but to keep one's temper, and not to rise to provocation. That was the best policy and he was pleased and even rather proud that he had succeeded in it so well today.

"Ought I to see anyone before I go?" he asked when Jane told him that Rosamund had had enough of company and must rest now.

The girls consulted each other. Both of them expressed surprise that Mary Warley had not found some excuse for coming in during Robert's visit, and Jane was of the opinion that he should make some polite remarks to her before leaving the premises. Rosamund seemed reluctant to put him to any further ordeal.

In the end the problem solved itself. Robert found his way back to the hall, to be greeted by a white-haired woman in a blue overall who asked if he was Mr. Fenniman, and if so could he spare a moment to come up to Mrs. Warley's sitting-room. He followed her up the broad staircase to one of the front rooms on the first floor. It seemed to him to be even more luxuriously furnished than Rosamund's room and he noticed that it overlooked both the front drive and the tradesmen's entrance and therefore gave the occupant a good view of all the comings and goings at Willoughby House.

Mary Warley offered him tea, which he declined, saying that the nurse had given him some.

"Ah yes. Nurse Bates. You're a friend of hers, I gather?"

"That's right. She mentioned me to Miss Morgan, and Miss Morgan said she'd like me to visit her."

"An excellent nurse," said Mary. "Have you known her long?"

"Oh—about five or six years."

Probing, thought Robert, and decided to be perfectly courteous but not to give her any help. He felt more and more convinced that she had either been responsible, or had connived, at the attempt to keep him out of the house. Probably one of them had actually telephoned the cousin and told him to arrive at the same moment. The red-faced husband was a fool; here in this room was the brains. She was making an effort now to appear friendly, but he could not feel any warmth towards her.

Poor Rosamund. No wonder Jane had said that she was lonely and lacking in love, in spite of all her wealth. A female cousin who was cold and correct and a male cousin who was quite appalling. Would she not be better in the anonymous kindness of a hospital or nursing home? But apparently she loved her home and could not bear to leave it. Next time they would talk about it, and about her own childhood. She owed him some confidences in return for his having stripped off his shell for her and her alone.

"Are you in the medical line yourself?" Mary Warley was asking.

"No. I'm a lecturer in English literature."

For some reason or other this seemed to reassure her.

"Rosamund did a history degree," she said. "She got an upper second and wanted to go on to research work, but it was just at that time that her illness started. I sometimes think that it may have been aggravated by the shock of her mother's death. She took an overdose of drugs. They called it accident, but of course . . ."

She shrugged and left the sentence unfinished. Suicide, thought Robert, and wondered whether Jane knew. If so, wouldn't it make her doubt more and more whether great wealth brought happiness?

"I'm sorry," he muttered inadequately.

"And now this," said Mary. "We're really rather a tragic family, Mr. Fenniman."

Robert could think of nothing to say. The room was beginning to oppress him and Mary Warley's conversation made him uneasy. He longed to get out into the open and walk across the Heath and think of Rosamund, going over those first terrible and wonderful minutes again and again in his mind.

"There is little more to be done for her now except blood transfusions," Mary went on. "She goes into hospital every now and then to have them. And pain-killing drugs. There is pain, of course, but fortunately not excessive. Sedatives if necessary, naturally. Dr. Milton does not recommend a bone marrow transplant, but there is a new antileukaemia drug that my cousin has consented to try, and which will probably involve daily injections."

Why is she telling me this, wondered Robert. Was it to rub in the fact of Rosamund's fatal illness? Was it to make him see her as a clinical case and not as a rare and beautiful woman?

"I say this," said Mary as if reading his thoughts, "so that you don't think we are just being obstructive and difficult when we try not to let her overtire herself with visitors. She is so sweet-tempered that she is incapable of protecting herself so we have to do it for her."

"I quite understand," said Robert, "and I promise I won't stay too long when I come again. The nurse will tick me off if I do," he added with an attempt at lightness.

"She ought to do so," was the frowning reply, "but I sometimes wonder . . . I'm not for a moment criticizing your friend, Mr. Fenniman. As I said, I think she is an excellent nurse and a very bright and lively person. She has certainly cheered my cousin. But there might perhaps be a danger in being too lively—when a patient is so very weak—you see what I mean?"

Yes, thought Robert grimly, I see what you mean: you'd like to get rid of Jane. Aloud he said: "I'll tell her you're a bit worried about it, shall I?"

"Tactfully, please," begged Mary Warley. "I wouldn't want to upset her. She's such an excellent nurse and my cousin likes her so much."

After a few more remarks in praise of Jane he was released

at last to walk on the Heath in the evening spring sunshine. But he did not, as he had intended, immediately lose himself and then re-find himself in thoughts of Rosamund. Instead he found himself thinking about Mr. and Mrs. Warley and Cousin John and the whole set-up at Willoughby House. There seemed to him to be an air of threat, something almost sinister about the place. And it was not only because a girl was dying there.

Sinister? Threat? That implied danger. But who could possibly be in danger except Rosamund herself? That was quite obvious in any case. Rosamund was dying. Could somebody be planning to hasten her death?

Impossible. Those who expected to inherit her wealth could not have long to wait. And she must have decided long ago what she was going to do with it. And having decided, she would stand by her decision. Rosamund was the last person in the world to take pleasure in tormenting her friends and relations by threatening to cut them out of her will.

On the other hand, if someone were deeply to offend her . . .

Did Jane have any evidence that Rosamund might be in danger?

Suddenly Robert discovered that he had not the least desire to talk about Rosamund to Jane at all. Perhaps she would understand that he didn't want to. Jane could be surprisingly perceptive at times. That was why it was so strange that he had never felt able to let her see the full depths of his own personal hurt. Whereas with Rosamund . . .

Infinite compassion. That was what she possessed. A very

rare quality. Perhaps only saints, or those at a great crisis in their own lives, could attain it.

Robert walked on and on, down sandy paths to shady spots where the grass was still damp from last night's rain, and then up the hillside until he reached a place where he could look down upon London in the distance.

There he paused. The sense of threat and evil that had been haunting him cleared at last. His mind was free and open, full of the wonderful warmth of Rosamund's eyes and voice and the touch of her fingers on his hair. Soothing and healing, freeing him from the strain of years of holding down his own pain and fear. It was like a miracle, and alone up here, with London far away and only a few people strolling past and taking no notice of him, he was free to relish it to the full.

It was like an ecstasy, this adoration of Rosamund's understanding and compassion, and it was very short-lived.

But she's dying, said a voice as if from outside himself.

I know, he answered it; I've known that all along.

You knew it with your thoughts, returned the voice; you didn't feel it with your heart because it didn't matter to you. It does matter now.

"But she mustn't die!" Robert did not know that he was crying out loud. "I need her. I love her. She mustn't die!"

He felt a drop of water on his face, then another and then another. He had not noticed the storm clouds coming up behind the hill while in front of him the distant buildings still glinted in late sunlight.

The rain was torrential. He ran at first, primitive instinct driving him to seek shelter. After a while he became so soaked that he ceased to care. When he got to a road where there was a bus route he just went on walking. It didn't seem to matter where he was or where he went.

But the homing instinct must still have been functioning because an hour later Jane, having long since got back from work, opened the front door of their flat and exclaimed in a mixture of relief and horror.

"Robert! Thank God you've come. I've been worried to death not knowing where you were. You're absolutely drowned—you're shivering—you'll get pneumonia."

She dried him and dosed him and fussed him and nursed him, but she did not ask where he had been. And he did everything that she told him to and thanked her and apologized but did not say what he had been doing since they parted at Willoughby House several hours previously.

And the whole evening not a word was said between them about Rosamund.

6

"Mrs. Patterson," said Rosamund at around half-past eleven that evening.

"Yes, my dear?"

"I don't feel like going to sleep just yet. Will you stay and talk to me?"

"Of course."

"Fetch your knitting if you want to."

Angela Patterson laughed. "I can bear to be without it for once." Feverish, she thought as she turned the lamp so that it did not shine on Rosamund's face. Perhaps the recent improvement had been only a false dawn.

"Have you ever met Jane?" asked Rosamund presently.

"The new nurse? No. I only know her handwriting from the notes she leaves me about any medicines that you may have had during the day."

"How strange." Rosamund seemed to fall into a reverie. "Jane's coming tomorrow," she went on eventually, "although it's Saturday. But she must have a day off sometime, and I wondered if you'd be free to come Sunday instead of the two nights this weekend."

"I could do that," said Angela. "But what about the nights?"

"We can manage. Mrs. Warley will listen for the bell and come if I need any help during the night."

Was this a good sign or a bad? Angela Patterson could not decide.

"Dr. Milton approved of it," Rosamund went on. "Don't be offended, Mrs. Patterson, but you see I've felt for some time now that I don't need and certainly don't want so much nursing. I did when I last came back from hospital, and it's just gone on as things do. After all, I'm not exactly helpless and I can swallow a pill if I need it. And any injections can be done during the day. If only I could have a few hours when I had at least the illusion of feeling less watched, more independent, more normal! Of course it's only an illusion, but it's very precious. Can you understand, Mrs. Patterson?"

"Yes," said Angela. "I know what you mean."

To a certain type of person, the oppressiveness of never feeling completely alone is even worse than all the pain and discomfort of illness. That was what her husband used to say. But she still could not judge whether or not this was a hopeful sign. "I can swallow a pill if I need it." Or more than one pill. Hopelessly ill patients might be forgiven for wanting to hurry on the inevitable end. Was that the explanation for Rosamund's present rather disturbed state of mind?

Angela could never make up her mind on the rights and wrongs of such cases. She hoped she would never be put in a position to make a judgement. Life and death. Those who thought they knew the exact values of life and death were lucky people. Or else they were wicked people.

But Rosamund was talking again. "I want to tell you something because I know you won't tell anybody else and

I badly need some advice. But first of all—let me ask you something I've been meaning to for some time. Is there anything of mine that you would like to have when I die?"

It was a simple and serious question and deserved a similar reply.

"I've always admired your writing-desk," said Angela after a moment's thought. "The wood is so beautiful."

"Thank you," said Rosamund. "If only everybody would be so honest and so sensible. I'll get Mr. Quick to add it to your legacy."

"I would rather have it instead of a legacy."

"I have noted your comments, as they say. Now to my story. Did you know that at the time when they first diagnosed leukaemia there was a man with whom I was in love and he with me and we'd almost decided to get married?"

Angela shook her head. "No. I didn't know."

"Not many people do. It's better forgotten. He offered to go ahead in spite of the diagnosis but I wouldn't let him. I knew he couldn't take it. He was a research chemist. Very brilliant. The next few years were vital to his future. He had to be free to go anywhere, take on anything that he was asked to do. He could do without an invalid wife. Even a very wealthy one."

"But surely—"

"No. Please don't get indignant. I'm not bitter now. I was very bitter at the time. Of course I wanted him to throw away his prospects and devote himself to me. Who wouldn't? Anyway that's all over and I'm only telling you in order to make sense of the next bit. I've known a number of men since then who would willingly have gone through a form of marriage with me, leukaemia and all, and even put on a very good show of caring for me and supporting me. Perhaps some of them really did care for me."

"I'm sure they did," broke in Angela.

"Perhaps I've been wrong in thinking that the inheritance was the chief attraction. But I couldn't love them, so there was no question of it."

She was silent for a while and Angela waited patiently, wondering if this were all or if there was more to come.

"This afternoon," said Rosamund after a while, "I met a man whom I could love. And if he had been around when they diagnosed leukaemia I know he would not have wanted to escape and I would not have wanted him to. So you can imagine what a state of mind that's put me into, Mrs. Patterson. If I'd been well I would have flung myself into some feverish activity just to calm myself down."

"Sedation," suggested Angela tentatively.

"Yes, I'll get you to give me a shot of diomorphine when I've finished talking. I really do need it. Let me tell you the full complications. You'll just have to take it that there was this instant recognition between us. If I'm wrong about that —well, I just know that I'm not wrong. Even now, with me having maybe two or three months to live, there might still be something that we could give each other. But he isn't free. He hasn't got a wife but he has got a very permanent girl. They obviously live together although I've not been told so."

"You know the girl?"

"Yes. It's Jane."

"But why," began Angela.

"Why does she bring him to see me if she thinks there is any danger that he and I might fall in love at first sight?

The answer is that she didn't think so. Would you, in her place?"

"No, of course not," said Angela.

"It's part of her campaign to brighten me up and get me interested in people and things outside. Nurses often do it. Usually it means bringing along their children so that the patient can see a bit of young life—at least that's the theory! Of course they like showing off their families but the intention is good and quite innocent on the whole. You must know about this sort of thing, Mrs. Patterson."

"Yes, of course I do."

"It's you who are the exception," said Rosamund. "Sometimes it's a husband or boy-friend. Everybody is very polite and the nurse and I have something more to chat about. But that it could result in this—"

Angela Patterson was both puzzled and alarmed. That something overwhelming had happened to Rosamund there could be no doubt. In other circumstances it might have been just the spur to life that she had so hoped for for the girl. But as things were it seemed to spell nothing but danger and despair.

"Did Jane notice anything?" she asked.

"I don't know. We'd—sort of calmed down by the time she came in. There was a slightly uneasy feeling but no worse than it often is when people are introduced to each other, and it was partly due to my cousin having been very rude to him when he arrived. After he'd gone Jane was just as usual, said she was delighted that we liked each other and that she knew he'd be looking forward to the chess. I don't know what she really felt. I like her enormously but she's very difficult to understand. He feels that too. Yet another bond." She closed her eyes for a moment or two before going on. "He's to come again Sunday afternoon. Jane won't be here. But I hope you will be. After that please could you advise me. If it goes on like this, that we both feel this way, even though of course there's no future in it, aren't we being disloyal to Jane and ought I to tell him not to come?"

"Couldn't you leave that for him and Jane to decide?" suggested Angela gently. "After all, in the last resort he is the one who must make the decision."

"I suppose so. I can't talk any more. Can I have that knock-out shot now, please?"

Long after Rosamund had sunk into a drugged sleep Angela Patterson sat by her bed. The knitting lay untouched. Angela's thoughts were in almost as great a tumult as Rosamund's. If this were true—wasn't it just the spur for life that was needed? Love could work miracles. Anything might happen. If only the man were the right sort.

But he was not free. Even a healthy girl might find that this led to a struggle between love and conscience that was very exhausting. For anyone not in good health the strain would be intolerable. How could Rosamund cope with it? It would not give her life; it would destroy her even more surely than the cancer which was slowly killing her now. What devilish fate could have put her into this position? A sort of torture of Tantalus, the treasure just beyond her reach.

And yet there might be a little happiness of a sort. Yes, she would meet the young man and decide for herself, and perhaps it would all look clearer then. Perhaps the girl would not mind giving him up so very much. After all, it could not be for long. But was not she, Angela Patterson, hoping that it *would* be for long? And what on earth would Rosamund's relations think if they knew about it?

At eight o'clock the following morning Rosamund was still fast asleep. Mary Warley came into the nurses' room, as was her custom, to enquire what sort of night the patient had had.

"Very peaceful," replied Nurse Patterson calmly. "She tells me that you are going to try to dispense with night nursing for a couple of nights and that I should come in Sunday for the day."

"That's right. If it would be convenient to you. It's her own wish. She's been saying for some time that she doesn't really need a night nurse and Dr. Milton agreed to the experiment."

"You'll answer her bell if need be?"

"Naturally. I sleep in the room above this. I looked after her before the last spell in hospital."

Mary Warley walked over to the medicine cupboard and added: "Perhaps you'll be good enough to let me know the present position on medication."

"You wouldn't rather ask the day nurse when she leaves this evening?"

"No, thank you, Mrs. Patterson. I prefer to ask you."

"All right." Angela opened the cabinet. "You have a key?"

"Yes."

"These are the sleeping tablets. She usually has two."

I suppose this is all right, thought Angela as she went through the contents of the cabinet. After all, if one can't trust the person in charge of the house . . . and she has looked after Rosamund before . . . and she is primarily responsible, even when I or one of the others is on the premises . . . but all the same . . .

"Prednesol," she went on. "These tablets are soluble. Here's the latest antileukaemia drug that Dr. Milton is trying. Daily injections for the next two weeks. Here's the hypodermic—but the day nurse will be attending to the injections."

In any case, thought Angela as she continued her steady explanations, somebody or other has to be in charge of Rosamund's medicines, and if not Mrs. Warley, then it must be the day nurse when I'm not here. And this particular day nurse—well, if what Rosamund says is true, then she has as good a motive for hastening on the death as the cousin has. So there was no help for it. The only solution was for Rosamund to be in hospital, and Angela Patterson decided that it was now time to carry out her resolution of talking to Mr. Quick, even if it meant breaking Rosamund's confidence.

The outcome of the subsequent conversation was that Mr. Quick was sitting with Rosamund when Robert arrived on Sunday afternoon. The Warleys had gone on a duty visit to Mary's mother, and it was Angela who answered the door.

The house felt very peaceful. The disturbing sense of tension and threat was absent. Supposing Rosamund were well, thought Robert as the middle-aged woman in the nurse's uniform greeted him kindly; she would then take charge in her own house, she would walk down those stairs dressed in jeans and a sweater, or perhaps in a crimson dress, and she would say, Hi there, Robert, and then—

No. There would be no "and then." Rosamund Morgan, young and healthy and very beautiful and very rich would have no use for Robert Fenniman at all.

"How is she?" he asked.

"Looking forward to seeing you. Go ahead. You know the way."

There could hardly have been a greater contrast to his reception on the previous occasion, but the coming into Rosamund's room felt just the same. Like coming home. Like journey's end.

She was sitting in one of the yellow armchairs and she turned and held out both arms to him. He did not see Mr. Quick standing near the bookshelves that covered the inside wall of the room. He ran straight to Rosamund's chair and knelt down by her side and caught her hands and kissed them. She bent her head forward and her lips brushed his hair.

Mr. Quick moved silently towards the door and closed it silently behind him. He had not intended to eavesdrop or to spy, but perhaps it was just as well that it had happened this way. No amount of talking and discussion with either Robert or Rosamund or both of them together could have brought him greater conviction of the truth of what he had been told than these few looks and gestures had brought. It reminded Mr. Quick, an opera-lover, of the death of Mimi at the end of *La Boheme*.

He sat down on an upright chair by the table in the nurses' room and rested his head on his hand.

"I fear you were right, Mrs. Patterson."

"About Rosamund and this young man?"

"Yes." He drooped and sagged over the table, looking suddenly every bit of his eighty years, and more. "But please don't ask me what we are to do about it because I haven't the least idea." He rubbed at his eyes as if his head ached. "All these years I have worried over her and watched over her and tried to think of everything I could do to bring her help and comfort and to save her trouble and distress, but I never dreamt, I never even dared to hope, not for one moment did I ever imagine that something like this could happen to her."

But that's not true, he thought as he gripped his head with both hands and stared at the mottled grey formica top of the table; I have imagined it, I have dreamed of it. Of another human being who would love Rosamund not for her money but for herself; not for the memory of how she used to be, but for herself as she is now, frail and wasted and near the end. I prayed for somebody who would truly mourn her and I knew I would not fail to recognize the true sight and sound of mourning and of love.

Then why was he not pleased that his prayer had been granted? Because he had thought only of Rosamund, not of the other, the owner of the voice he had so longed to hear. For whoever loved Rosamund now was doomed to suffer. This Rudolph could not throw off his role when the curtain came down but must go on living and feeling and grieving. And although Mr. Quick told himself that it was absurd to imagine that he was in any way responsible for the situation, he still could not throw off the totally irrational notion that it was in some way or another his own fault.

"I don't see that we can do anything at all," said Angela Patterson. "Except perhaps try to persuade Rosamund to go into hospital or nursing home. Robert could visit her there and it would be less embarrassing for him and Jane. And he wouldn't have to put up with the rudeness of Rosamund's relations."

"She won't go," replied Mr. Quick. "She says she loves this house and she wants to watch the garden blossom in the spring and walk out there with Robert when the sun gets warm enough. Is that so much to ask?"

He looked up at Angela Patterson and the nurse shook her head. No, it was not so very much to ask.

"I was afraid you might not come," said Rosamund.
"Why were you afraid?"
"Because." She drew back a little. "Because I'm—"
She broke off, and when she spoke again it was to ask: "What did you do after you left me the other day?"
"Said goodbye to your cousin Mary Warley and was sort of granted permission to visit you again and after that I walked on Hampstead Heath for hours to try to sort things out."
"And where did the things end up?"
"In the same sort of muddle they started in. How could I love Jane—because I do most truly love Jane and have done for years—and yet feel when I saw you that I'd been searching for you always and that you were my peace and my hope and my key and my security. Can one love two people at once?"
"It seems that one can. Was that the end of the sorting?"
"No. Only the beginning. The more I tried to see it clearly the more I realized that what I felt for Jane was getting dimmer and dimmer and dying away and what I felt for you was getting stronger and brighter and—"
"And then?" prompted Rosamund softly.
"And then I suddenly remembered your illness and it was as if somebody had hit me over the head and I began crying and raving like mad. All alone up on Hampstead Heath, shaking my fist at the heavens. And then something really

did hit me on the head." He smiled up at her from where he was now sitting at her feet. "Rain. It came down in sheets."

"Robert! You weren't out through all that storm?"

"Through every last bit of it. I got home looking like a drowned rat and Jane put me to bed and plied me with hot drinks, and I don't think I've even so much as sneezed. Otherwise I might really have hesitated about coming, because the last thing you want is to catch my colds."

She made no reply but he noticed her change of expression.

"Rosamund, my love, what have I said to upset you?"

"Nothing." She smiled. "Go on. Tell me more about Jane. She didn't say anything about your adventure when she was here yesterday. In fact she said very little about you at all. Perhaps she was still trying to pretend that you two don't live together."

"Oh yes. I'd quite forgotten. She didn't want you to know. But I knew you'd guessed."

"And has she guessed that you feel this way about me?"

"I think so. She's playing it very cool."

"She has no need to worry. She has only to wait. Just like everybody else."

Robert got up from the floor and sat on the arm of the chair and held her very gently. She was as frail and as trembling as a captured bird.

"Not everybody," he said. "I'm not waiting. If you are dead I no longer want to live. That's what I shouted aloud up there in the storm on the Heath."

There was silence for a while and then she said: "Poor Robert."

"Isn't there any hope at all? Faith-healers? A pilgrimage to Lourdes?"

"Would you like me to try a faith-healer? I will if you'd like me to."

"But you'd rather not?"

"I—I think I'm frightened. I think I'm frightened of hope. Can you understand that, Robert?"

"Very well indeed. The first and most important lesson that I learnt in my life was how to live without hope."

Presently she said: "If I feel I can bear to try a faith-healer I will let you know. Mrs. Patterson will arrange it. She knows somebody. So can we forget it now? Did you manage the chess problem?"

"Eventually. With difficulty. Would you like me to show you?"

He explained the moves and Rosamund exclaimed in delighted understanding and then they talked again. Time passed, each minute lived purely in itself, without thought or fear or hope of the next.

At last Rosamund said: "If you want some tea I think you're going to have to go and fetch it. Mrs. Patterson seems tactfully to have disappeared."

She told him where to go. He came back with a tray and a message from Mrs. Patterson to say that she was going out for a little while. "Looks as if we've got the house to ourselves," he added.

"How lovely."

He agreed enthusiastically and tried to recapture the timeless mood. It would not come. Time seemed to be rushing by and the fear of its passing only increased the speed. It was racing towards the moment when other people would return, the nurse, the relations and the house would no longer belong to Rosamund and himself; racing towards the moment when he must leave, racing towards the inevitable end.

"Next time you come," said Rosamund, "you will find me up and dressed and I am going to ask you to help me out onto the lawn. To stand on grass. Have you ever thought what a wonderful sensation that is? The firmness and security of earth and the softness of its living covering."

"I've known it without thinking about it," he replied. "But now whenever I walk on grass I shall think of you. Not that I'm not thinking of you all the time."

"And I of you."

The peace and the freedom would not return, but at least they were rushing through time together and by stating a day and an hour for their reunion could gain the illusion of having time under their control.

"Wednesday," said Robert.

"Wednesday," repeated Rosamund. The very unit that measured time had become a magic word.

"I'll be coming again on Wednesday," said Robert to Angela Patterson who was waiting for him in the nurses' room.

"Then we shall meet again. I have just had a telephone call from the agency to ask if I will take over the day nursing."

"Day nursing?" It was a second or two before the full implications of this information sank in.

"Didn't your friend Jane tell you that she had asked to be transferred to another job?"

"Oh yes. Of course."

Had Jane told him? Had he been so abstracted that he had not taken it in? Or had she been afraid to tell him for fear of the discussion that must follow? Or just thought it easier for them both if he were to find out in this way that she would no longer be nursing Rosamund? He was inclined to think that Jane was trying to make things less difficult between them, and one day, when this present madness was over, he might be able to show her that he was grateful.

But for now, well they must just go on living together and being careful towards each other and, as Rosamund had said, all Jane had to do was wait. She might even get some money, since Rosamund was both fond of her and guilty towards her. But that was one of the things that was best not even thought about, and certainly not talked about. In fact there was an alarming number of things that must not be mentioned to either Rosamund or Jane or to neither of them, and it was lucky, thought Robert, that his life had taught him not only the dangers of hope, but also the need for caution.

That casual remark about not wanting Rosamund to catch his cold, for instance. It was the sort of thing one said unthinkingly. But to Rosamund the catching of a cold would not be a temporary annoyance of greater or lesser degree: it would literally be a matter of life or death, because her illness left her with no resistance at all, not even to the slightest infection.

The thought was terrifying, as if one were carrying the greatest treasure in an eggshell.

Robert walked down the front drive of Willoughby House so deep in thought that he did not see a man get out of a small car that was parked outside the gates. Mr. Quick had to call his name twice before he looked up.

7

"You're back early," said Jane, looking up from the book she was reading.

"Mr. Quick drove me home."

"That was kind. He's a very kind old man, I think."

"Does he live alone, do you know?" asked Robert.

"I think so. He's a widower."

They discussed Raymond Quick cautiously and conscientiously and managed not to mention Rosamund. Then Robert had an inspiration.

"Has the agency found you a job for tomorrow?" he asked as casually as he could.

"Hospital supply," she replied in the same tone of voice. "For a couple of weeks. It'll be rather fun to go back and hear all the gossip."

He felt too grateful and relieved to leave any room for wondering whether she was playing some deep game of her own.

"What are you reading?" he asked.

"Hardy." She held up the paperback for him to read the title: *Jude the Obscure*. "There's certain similarities between you and Jude," she said with a hint of her old teasing self.

"Naive? Vulnerable?"

"Possibly."

She returned to her book and Robert began to collect together the books and papers that he would be using for his next day's teaching.

"Oh, by the way," he said, "I meant to tell you. My American student, Mike, has chosen his set books for A levels. We're definitely doing the Henry James. It's not *Washington Square*, it's *The Wings of the Dove*. I've never read it and it looks tough going. So any help you can give me will be gratefully received."

"Of course, darling," she murmured, barely glancing up from her reading.

Robert was a little disappointed that she had not immediately followed up this fresh move of his to keep their conversation on the safe subject of literary criticism, but this homecoming had been so very much less difficult than he had expected that the predominant feeling was still one of relief.

Several days passed in this manner. Wednesday afternoon was exceptionally warm for the time of year and he was welcomed to Willoughby House by a smiling Nurse Patterson.

"Mrs. Warley apologizes for not coming to speak to you," she said, "but she is resting. She is answering Rosamund's bell at night now, you know, and although there is not much to be done, it seems to have disturbed her sleeping pattern."

The misgivings that Robert still felt about Rosamund being in the care of her cousin were soon outweighed by the happy excitement of Angela Patterson.

"You're going to have a surprise," she said as they approached the door of Rosamund's room. "Prepare yourself."

He was not surprised and yet he had not really believed it possible.

Rosamund was standing by the open french window, leaning against the frame. She was wearing dark green slacks and a white angora shawl round her shoulders. She was looking out at the garden as they opened the door and for a moment Robert saw her as behind the footlights on a stage, remote and unattainable. Then he thought: this is how she must have been before her illness, tall and slim and graceful in stillness and in movement.

"Hurry up," she cried. "I can't stand here much longer."

He ran forward and put an arm round her and she leaned against him and they stepped down onto the flagstones.

"Don't talk," he urged. "Save your breath. Then tell me afterwards."

She pressed his hand in agreement.

They moved very slowly forward onto the grass and towards the copper beech tree, around whose trunk the daffodils and yellow crocuses grew. And then they turned to the shrubs, and she reached up to touch the bright green leaf-buds on a lilac bush and the spiky twigs of forsythia. At one point she drooped so much that Robert feared she would fall, and he wondered whether he ought to carry her to all the places she wished to go. Then he remembered how much she had longed to feel the grass beneath her feet and he decided against it.

It was worth it. Even if it killed her. It was for Rosamund to decide.

She drew him towards a corner of the lawn where an old swing hung from a branch of a horse chestnut tree, touched one of the ropes and smiled at him.

That's where she played as a child, he thought as he smiled back.

Then she pointed to an old garden shed, dark green woodwork with ivy straggling over the roof. Another memory, he thought. As they stood looking at the shed its door opened and an old man came out carrying a rake. He stopped dead when he saw Rosamund and stared as if he had seen a ghost.

"George," whispered Rosamund and seemed to want to say more but failed.

"Every time I go near your window," said the old man, "I think to myself, maybe that window will open and out she comes. Maybe come spring, I say to myself." He rubbed his eyes. "And it's happened. And here she is."

Within the support of his arm Robert felt Rosamund tremble.

"Yes, here she is," he said, "but I think it's enough for the first time and we'd better go back now."

He had to say it. Rosamund was on the point of collapse. Flowers she could cope with, but not the presence of human emotion. But it broke the spell. They were no longer walking in Paradise. She was a desperately sick woman venturing for the first time for months into the fresh air, and it was his responsibility to bring her safely in again.

He scarcely believed she could manage it, but she did. Mrs. Patterson was waiting and with a mixture of great sadness and great relief he relinquished Rosamund to her expert hands.

"Go and make tea," said Angela. "I'll get her into bed and then you can talk a little, but you'd better not stay too long."

They were right back in the invalid routine again. It had

to be, but it was like prison after a glimpse of freedom. And if I feel like this, thought Robert as he switched on the kettle in the nurses' room, how much more must Rosamund? How right she was to be afraid of hope. What had he done to her—he and Jane together, for it was Jane who had started it all. Kindness or cruelty? It was pointless to try to judge. There was no turning back now.

It came almost as a reassurance to see Rosamund back in bed, lying as she had been when he first saw her.

"Poor old George," were the first words she spoke. "I feel that someone ought to go and comfort him. He's known me since I was four years old, you see."

"I'll go," said Angela. "Where shall I find him?"

Rosamund thought for a moment. Or perhaps she was summoning up the strength to speak again. "By the camellias. That's where we used to have long conversations when I was a child."

After Angela had gone she said to Robert: "He used to call me the Lady of the Camellias. And you know what happened to *her*."

A little later she added: "If it were consumption I could now be cured."

He made no comment. There was a threat of hysteria in her voice. If it came, he would not know what to do. He longed for Mrs. Patterson's return. For a moment or two he even longed for Jane.

Rosamund sipped sweet tea and seemed to gain a little strength. "Thank you, Robert. Wasn't that lovely?"

"Lovely. Did the grass come up to expectations?"

"It did. The scent of newly-cut grass."

"And dew on the grass."

"And all the insect life it contains."

"I wonder why poets haven't written of the glory of grass?"

Rosamund gave a little gasp of laughter. "Maybe because of its slang connotations. Would you say it's a ruined word, like 'gay'?"

It was amazing. She seemed to have come right up out of the exhaustion and to be eager to talk again. Mrs. Patterson didn't seem to think it so very strange, but she told Robert firmly when the time had come to go. At the front door she said as he was leaving: "That went very well. She stood up to it better than I'd expected."

"You don't mean you think—oh please don't say it if it's just meaningless medical brightness! Please tell me what you really believe. Is there any chance? Of anything at all? Could she live through the summer? Could she come for a drive round the Heath?"

"I don't just believe—I *know*—that there is always the possibility of some degree of recovery. Miracles have even been known to happen in which the recovery appears complete—even after three years no relapse."

"But that's in general. I mean with Rosamund."

"She's got something to live for now. That makes a great difference," said Angela beaming at him.

He did not know whether to be grateful to her or not. Each time the parting from Rosamund became more difficult to endure. It was like death.

Upstairs, in Mary Warley's sitting-room, three people were grouped in chairs round the open window.

"He's gone," said Bill Warley, whose seat commanded the best view of the front gate.

John Aylmer got up and walked about the room. "I don't

know what you hope to gain, Mary, by letting this fellow take over Rosamund like this. It strikes me as risky in the extreme. Next thing we know she'll have got better and married him and bang go all our hopes for ever."

"I say, old boy, that's going a bit far, isn't it?" said Bill Warley. "I mean it's no good being hypocritical and pretending we don't want Rosamund's money, but after all—I mean to say—after all she's terribly ill, poor girl. I mean one can't talk about the possibility of her getting better as being a frightful tragedy, can one now? Even between ourselves. It's just not on."

John Aylmer gave him a contemptuous look and made no reply.

"There is not the faintest possibility of Rosamund making even a partial recovery," said Mary steadily. "The very most that can be expected is a short remission, and at this stage that doesn't mean recovery. It means a pause in the overall deterioration, but with the usual ups and downs. Some good days, some bad days. Does it really make all that difference to us whether we inherit in two months' time or in six months' time?"

"Speak for yourself," said John. "Personally I could do with it now."

Mary looked up at him. In her face was something of the contempt that he himself had shown for Bill. And yet am I any better, she asked herself: have I not thought again and again how convenient it would be if Rosamund were to die quickly and painlessly and very soon? Have I not jumped eagerly at the chance to do some of the nursing myself again so that I have every possibility of observing her . . .

But I could never do it, she thought; not directly. I could perhaps bring myself to leave a lethal dose of pills within her reach if she was very depressed; I might allow her to do things beyond her strength that might well have drastic consequences, like this crazy walk in the garden today. But deliberately to give the wrong injection or the wrong tablets —no, never. And whether that makes me a coward, or just saves me from eternal damnation I really don't know.

"What do you propose we should do, John?" she said aloud. "Murder our cousin?"

"Oh don't be such a bloody fool. Of course I'm not suggesting anything of the sort, although I should think it ought to be easy enough for you, with your knowledge of nursing, and having every opportunity to do the job quickly and undetected."

He glanced at her and she glanced back. Bill began to bluster again and they took no notice of him.

"I am not a hypocrite," said Mary icily. "I don't pretend that I would have taken on the job of looking after this house if it had not been for the hope of increasing my inheritance from the Morgan estate, but I am not in any desperate hurry to receive it. And neither is Bill," she added as an afterthought before going on. "I've always been fond of Rosamund and I am very sorry for her."

"Of course, of course," said Bill. "Terrible thing, this illness, terrible."

He uttered the words; it was Mary who, on this occasion at least, was speaking the truth. A woman without imagination and with little warmth of character, she nevertheless found herself moved by Rosamund's plight. And these last few nights, when she had attended to the girl's needs, had served to increase her compassion rather than to strengthen the temptation. If only she could be sure that her inheritance was safe and that these dangerous newcomers would not steal it from her. That was all that Mary Warley wished for. Secure of her inheritance, she would look after Rosamund conscientiously and with as much warmth as her nature was capable of, right up to the end.

So she believed. John Aylmer thought differently.

"So it's to be a mercy killing," he sneered.

"There is not going to be any killing at all, and I strongly advise you to stop talking about it," said Mary sharply. "If Rosamund were to die unexpectedly you could find yourself in serious trouble."

"Me? What could I do? I don't have a key to the medicine cabinet."

"Haven't you? Didn't you get a duplicate made at the time you got so pally with that little blonde nurse who used to come?"

"I don't know what you are talking about," said John.

"All right. We'll forget it. I'm just warning you. That's all. To revert to your question about Robert Fenniman. I too should much prefer him not to come and see Rosamund, but I can see no way to prevent it. I have tried legitimate methods but without success. Your method of being offensive at the front door—" and she included both men in her scornful glance "—is just too stupid for words and can only make things more difficult. If you go on like that you're going to get Raymond Quick on the warpath and then we really shall be at risk. I've gone to considerable trouble to soothe the young man down and I believe I've succeeded, and so far no harm is done. Our best ally is Dr. Milton. He was willing to believe that Jane Bates was not having a good effect on Rosamund's condition, but the girl solved the problem herself by resigning the job. The young man is a tougher proposition. Dr. Milton can't be persuaded to discourage the visits. I have a suspicion that Raymond Quick has been talking to him."

Mary got up from her chair as if bringing the meeting to a close but continued to talk.

"We have to remember that we are not in a strong position. Raymond never misses a trick. If we show too much impatience we will only be weakening ourselves. I shall keep a close watch and take what action I can if it seems advisable to do so."

"And meanwhile Ros cuts us all out of her will and leaves the whole damn lot to this bloody schoolmaster," said John Aylmer.

"That is unlikely in the extreme. She has strong family feelings and it would be wise not to offend them. And in such an event we would have Raymond Quick on our side. He is just as alive to the dangers of fortune-hunters as we are ourselves, and he has a great influence over Rosamund."

"Silly old bugger," muttered John.

"I'd like to have my room to myself now," said Mary. "I've got rather a headache."

Outside the door of her room the two men looked at each other. Then John jerked his head in the direction of the stairs and Bill followed him down and through the front door into the garden. They walked round the side of the house and stopped to talk under the horse chestnut tree from which hung Rosamund's old swing.

John sat down on it and moved gently to and fro. Bill stood a couple of yards away.

"We've got to do something at once," said John.

"What do you mean?"

"You know perfectly well what I mean. We can't rely on Mary."

"But what can we do?"

"Have you nothing to suggest?" John got up off the swing and gave it a violent push which sent the ropes winding round and round each other. Then he took Bill by the arm and walked him away.

"Give it some thought," he said in a low voice. "I'm going to have to depend on you to carry it out. You're in a better position than I am, being actually in the house."

"There's no reason why you shouldn't come and stay here for a while if you want to," said Bill with a little spurt of petulance.

"I haven't the slightest desire to immure myself in this morgue. Besides, it would look suspicious. Ray Quick knows that I loathe the place."

"You wouldn't mind having it to sell."

"Neither would Mary. But she'll find she doesn't even get the house if she goes on like this."

"I don't know what you're talking about," said Bill.

John's grip of his arm tightened. "You're becoming a bore, Bill. If Mary won't do the job then you'll have to do it yourself. You're the only other person who has the opportunity."

"I haven't got any opportunity for anything. It's all I can do to get out to the pub. Mary watches me like a hawk."

"She's not watching you now," said John, "and we are quite safe from interruption."

"I'm not going to murder Rosamund," said Bill.

"Nobody's asking you to. What pain-killer is she taking now?"

"Prednesol, but—"

"Would you recognize the bottle?"

They had come round the corner of the house again. Bill suddenly pulled his arm away. "Why don't you do your own dirty work?" he asked in a high voice.

"Nobody's talking about dirty work."

"You are. You're talking about killing Rosamund."

"Nobody is killing Rosamund. She is dying in any case. It could be sooner and it could be later. If she catches a cold, which she might well do after exposing herself to the outside air when she should have been keeping warm indoors, then the death will certainly be sooner. It would also be sooner if she were to fall subject to any other minor complaint that most people would scarcely notice. Do you understand me now?"

"You're talking about giving her an overdose, but that would be—"

"—not murder. Attempted suicide perhaps?"

"But why should Rosamund kill herself?" asked Bill.

"Most people would say she had very good reason. Are you frightened, Bill?"

"Of course I'm not frightened. I just don't see how I can get hold of the drugs, that's all."

"Don't you? Would you like me to tell you?"

John took his arm again and they walked back across the lawn.

It was a very beautiful evening. The sky was clear behind the still leafless branches of the great trees bordering the lawn and the blackbirds were singing and everywhere around them were the scents and sounds and urgency of the spring. The two men walking over the grass saw and heard nothing. Each was occupied with his own private vision: pieces of printed paper, figures in a bank balance, zero added to zero at the end of the line, wealth upon wealth.

Mary Warley lay on her bed upstairs. She had always suffered from headaches, but recently they had become much worse. The tablet that she had swallowed was at last beginning to take effect. In another ten minutes she would be able to get up and start preparing the evening meal. Grilled sole, and she wanted to try out a new sauce. It soothed her to recite the ingredients in her mind. She knew that she would be creating it for her own satisfaction alone, because nobody else in this house would appreciate its subtle flavour. Bill didn't care what he ate as long as he got enough of it, and in any case Mary had long since lost any desire to give any pleasure to Bill. Poor Rosamund might appreciate it if she had any appetite, but as likely as not she would want nothing but a milk drink and some fruit. And Mrs. Patterson would refuse the offer of a meal. As if she was afraid that I was going to poison her, thought Mary.

The head began to throb again. It always got worse when her thoughts started to run along these lines. John Aylmer. He would probably enjoy her cooking but she hoped he would not stay for the meal. She had never liked him. All show and no substance. What had he ever done to deserve his inheritance? At least she herself would have worked for it. She had never liked taking something for nothing.

John would never work for anything. He would talk about it for ever but never take any action. Just like Bill. What a pair they were! All this stupid talk about hastening on Rosamund's death. Neither of them would ever have the courage and strength of will to carry it through. She herself was the only one who possessed the courage and she was not going to do it. Listening to those two talking in that disgusting manner had made her more certain than ever that she was not going to do it.

If only that wretched nurse had not brought this young man into the house and Rosamund had not taken to him in such a big way. It was Robert Fenniman who was the problem, not poor Ros. She had made no recent change to her will: Mary was quite sure of that. Perhaps they were setting about the problem the wrong way. Perhaps they ought to try to deal with him more openly instead of all this spying and suspicion. Perhaps a direct appeal . . . He seemed a decent hard-working young man, a great deal more respectworthy, in Mary Warley's code, than Cousin John. But the money was a great temptation, and he must be hoping for some of it because why else should he be hanging round Rosamund when he had his own girl-friend?

His own girl-friend!

Mary got up off the bed with a speed that only a minute ago would have seemed impossible. How on earth could she have been so blind? Of course that was the answer. Nurse Bates must surely be wanting to separate Robert from Rosamund. But no: supposing they were in it together? Nurse Bates to get a foothold in the house, bring in her accomplice, a personable and appealing young man, and then withdraw and leave him to get on with the job. It seemed the right solution and yet Mary felt that it didn't fit. Rosamund didn't fall for that sort of trick, and as far as Mary could judge, Robert looked as if he might really be in love with her.

Like Romeo and Juliet. A doomed love.

For a moment Mary looked into a sphere of life that she had long since taught herself to ignore. It made her uneasy. She didn't like to think about people being in love except as a given fact that had to be taken account of like all other facts.

All right. Supposing this young man really did care for Rosamund. That didn't mean that he didn't want her money, but it did mean that Jane Bates might feel very differently about it. Very jealous, to put it plainly. And Jane Bates was not the sort of girl to sit back quietly and watch a rival take over her man.

Mary walked over to the dressing-table and combed her hair. If only it could somehow be arranged that Jane Bates would take Robert away from Rosamund, that would solve everything. No one need commit any crime nor even contemplate such a measure. They would be right back in the position that they were in before Nurse Bates came into the house, and who could wish for anything more?

After Robert had left the enchanted castle he decided to walk home because he had not the patience to wait for a bus and it seemed a crime to get on an underground train on this beautiful evening. Leafy side roads gave way to busy main streets and then to rows of crumbling Victorian town houses.

He was barely conscious of his surroundings and yet at the same time he felt as if every step was taking him further away from Rosamund, not only in physical distance, but in every other way. They lived in different worlds, and the two worlds met only in those precious moments of complete understanding and unity.

These moments had only a present: they had no future.

Robert told himself that this did not matter. After all, one could only live in the present. In any case, there would probably be a nuclear holocaust and nobody at all would have a future.

Thus his mind reasoned, but everything else in and around him cried out against it. One could not hold to such thoughts at this season of the year. Even here, right in the heart of London, with bricks and concrete stretching away for miles on every side, one could feel the whole earth stirring and the great sense of anticipation in the air. The secret, subtle, overwhelming and irresistible coming of spring. And his own youth and health and strength were all a part of it and would not be denied.

When he was five minutes away from home the sense of being cut off from Rosamund was so intolerable that he went into a public telephone box and dialled the number of Willoughby House. If a man's voice answers, he thought, I'll ring off at once. But Mrs. Warley would surely tell him how she was. Or put him through to Nurse Patterson.

It was a long time before there was any answer. Robert stared down at the floor of the telephone box. There was dust and grime and bottle tops and cigarette ends and a used contraceptive and a smell of stale urine. And in just such a place, he suddenly thought, I myself began.

It was a strange thought, disturbing but not disgusting. I must tell Rosamund, he decided. She will understand just how strange it is.

The telephone was answered at last and with joy and relief Robert recognized Angela Patterson's voice.

"I don't know where everybody is," she said. "I'm speaking from the extension in the nurses' room."

"How is Rosamund?"

"Sleeping at the moment. She's none the worse for her walk. She'll wake up presently and have some supper. I'll tell her that you rang."

"Please. And give her my love. And say that I'm looking forward to our next walk together."

"I'll do that, Robert. And I'd like to thank you. For myself as well as for her."

After they had rung off Robert glanced down again at the floor of the telephone box. He pictured Rosamund's garden in his mind and thought confusedly that it was all the same really, it all came to the same thing in the end. Feeling much calmer now, comforted by Nurse Patterson's words, puzzled by his own train of thought, he walked slowly homewards.

To Jane.

They could not go on like this much longer. They would have to talk it out and face the truth. If it had been a matter of temporary unfaithfulness on either side, the whole thing would have blown up immediately and been over by now. But this was different and much more serious. If Rosamund were well, and wanted him, he would leave Jane tomorrow. It would be a horrible thing to do but he knew he would do it. Even now, in Rosamund's extreme weakness, she had given him more than Jane could ever do and he had responded as he had never been able to with Jane.

How could Jane not be hurt? And if she was not hurt, it must mean she no longer loved him. In which case why did she stick with him?

But then it was her doing in the first place, he thought irritably as he turned the key in the front door of their flat. It was Jane who had insisted on his meeting Rosamund and had actually said she was afraid she might be jealous and had made a joke of it. Why had she wanted him to meet Rosamund? Well, perhaps that was not so very strange. She had been excited by the wealth and the luxury and moved by the ghastly contrast between that and Rosamund's own fate and had wanted somehow to share this experience with Robert.

He became aware that the flat was very quiet. Jane must be working a long day at the hospital. It was a relief, and yet he would like to get their first greetings over so that he could judge her mood and decide whether or not this was the moment to talk things out.

The little sitting-room felt crowded and oppressive after the space and openness of Willoughby House. The view from the window was of laurel bushes, a narrow roadway, and a high brick wall on the other side, beyond which was railway land and the railway itself. For a second Robert saw it through Jane's eyes. Then he turned to look at the table on which books and papers and clutter always collected until it was cleared off for them to have their meals.

On a corner of the table was a sheet of paper held in place by one of Jane's favourite treasures, a Victorian glass paperweight. This was not part of the usual clutter. Robert put it aside and picked up the paper and saw Jane's handwriting.

"Mother is not very well," he read. "I don't think it's very serious but I thought I'd better go down to see her. The train service is rotten and I won't be able to get back tonight but I'll phone you first thing in the morning. Don't ring tonight. Unless it's terribly urgent. It'll only disturb her. Hope all well. Lots of love from Jane."

Robert put down the sheet of paper and replaced the paperweight. For a moment or two it was as if Rosamund

Morgan had never come into their lives. The crashing conflict in his mind of hope and fear and dread and doubt and guilt took on the unreality of a dream. Jane's mother ill, Jane worried about her—this was the normal waking life.

The two worlds remained uneasily balanced while he made himself a meal and marked the most urgent of the student essays that were lying on the table. He put them into his briefcase and sat for a while deep in thought. On the one side was the familiar world of the crowded little room and Jane's mother's illness. On the other side was everything that gave meaning to life and without which he himself could scarcely draw breath, without which he would be as lost as the abandoned infant on the floor of the telephone booth.

There was no resolving the conflict at this moment. He had better try to forget it and continue to catch up with his work. Tomorrow afternoon he was supposed to be tutoring Mike, and he had not yet read the novel that Mike was studying for his A level English exam.

Robert twisted round in the chair and reached out behind him to the table. *The Wings of the Dove* was at the top of a little pile of paperback classic authors. Maybe there was something to be said for losing oneself in the lives of fictional characters. At least it took one's mind off one's own problems.

The cover illustration portrayed a languishing lady on a sofa. Henry James drawing-room stuff, thought Robert. The reading was a tiresome duty. He did not anticipate that he would feel any interest or pleasure in the novel at all.

8

At two o'clock in the morning he read the last sentence.

He was not aware of any fatigue. His whole consciousness seemed to be one blaze of understanding and of fury. In the middle of it was a hard little nugget of reasoning which said: this must be a unique occasion, the one and only time when any reader has got through so indigestible a novel at a single sitting.

He swallowed some whisky without tasting it, made strong coffee and swallowed that. Then he smoked one cigarette after another, tried to walk about the flat, banged into furniture, sat down, got up again, and finally walked out into the road and raged up and down.

After a while reaction set in and he returned home and lay exhausted on his bed. No wonder Jane had run away. If she had been there five minutes ago he would have strangled her. But the danger had passed and would not arise again. She had had the sense to keep out of his way during the vital first reaction. Apparently it had dawned on her at last that these were real people she was playing with, not fictional characters in the control of their author. And real people did not always react as intended.

The man in the book had not turned in violent fury upon the heroine when he discovered her diabolical plot. Oh no.

He had gone along with it, with a certain amount of misgivings, and had then used it to blackmail her into sleeping with him. But that was in Victorian times, when things were different.

Differences of detail, but essentially the same story. A clever and attractive and ambitious young woman longs to be rich. She could make a rich marriage, but she loves a poor man, a young newspaper reporter. And into their lives comes an American heiress, a sweet gentle affectionate creature who is dying of an incurable disease. English society fusses and flatters her but all are asking the question: who gets the money?

Kate, the ambitious poor girl, conceives a plan whereby she can have both the man and the money. A stroke of genius, which leaves her free to befriend the rich girl without any suggestion that she is angling for a legacy. She isn't. It's the young man who is to receive the legacy and they are then to spend it together. The dying rich girl takes a liking to him. He can be charming enough if need be and she is craving for life and love. Just you carry on like that, says his clever Kate; you're making her happy, bringing a bit of joy into her last months on earth. And if she likes to acknowledge it, well, who will be the worse? It's neat, it's logical, it hurts nobody, it's even compassionate. It will add to the sum total of human good.

Young reporter falls for it, the poor sap. Gets into such a state of confusion he scarcely knows what he's doing any more. Kate's plot is going along swimmingly. Surely she's going to end up with both the man and the money?

But she hasn't reckoned with one thing. The poor worm's self-disgust. Raised to an intolerable pitch by the true nobility of the heiress, the dove of the title. He's supposed to make her fall in love with *him:* he's not supposed to develop any strong feelings for *her,* except a sort of impersonal compassion.

But he does. He can't help it. He comes to love the dying dove. And then she dies. And leaves him a fortune. But can he accept it? No.

And so on to the bitter, bitter end.

A simple but subtle, smooth yet terrifying story. Clever. Most horribly and convincingly clever. At what moment, Robert wondered, had the similarity of the situation inspired Jane? She'd been taking a great risk. A teacher of English literature knows something of most of the works of the great novelists. But she knew that this was an author whom he had never liked and would read only the minimum necessary for his work. And this was not one of the books usually studied. What a shock she must have had when he told her about his new American student! No wonder she had taken such a detailed interest in Mike's exams. And when he had actually told her the title of the set book. She must have known then that she was finished.

Or did she still think that she could get round him? Was she still dreaming, like Kate, of having both the man and the money? Perhaps one ought to be flattered that a woman could go to such lengths not to lose you.

And what was to be the bitter end of the Jane and Robert and Rosamund story? As the night wore on the spell of the novel began to fade and Robert was able to take some stock of his own position. At least there was this small comfort: unlike the man in the novel, he had no complicity in the plot. He had been an ignorant and innocent tool. Thus far his conscience was clear. He knew now, and he had the power to act. Not to undo the feeling that he had for

Rosamund and she had for him: that was irreversible, and all of them must suffer for it.

On the emotional side there was nothing to be done, but on the financial side it was not too late. Should he speak to Rosamund herself? No. She might well suspect Jane of ulterior motives, but she certainly did not suspect himself. There was perfect trust between them. Even to mention her wealth would ruin it, completely destroy whatever little remained to them of frail joy and peace together. Not Rosamund. Raymond Quick was the answer. Robert decided to tell him everything. And to ring the college in the morning and say he was called away on urgent business and could not teach that day. He would make the time up to Mike and the others later in the week. This day was for real: fiction must wait.

The telephone bell woke him from a short and troubled sleep.

"Hullo, darling," said Jane's voice, falsely bright. "Did you find my note?"

"Yes. How's your mother?"

"Not too bad. It's only a cold. I may be coming back today."

The anxiety in her voice came clearly over the line. She was desperate to know whether he had guessed, dreading his reactions, hoping against all reason and against all experience of him that he would not care too much.

"Then we can talk this evening," said Robert calmly.

"Will you be late back?"

"I'm not going into college. There's some urgent business I have to attend to."

"Oh my God." It was a half-stifled exclamation. She went on more firmly: "Robert, you're not going to—"

She broke off, then added: "I can't talk now. Mum will get worried. And Uncle keeps coming in and out of the room."

"There's no need to talk now. When you get back. What train are you catching?"

"Oh—two-thirty. I'll probably get to Victoria about quarter to four."

"Right. Around half-past four. I'll be through with everything and be home by then."

"Robert, you're not—"

Her voiced failed again. It sounded as if she was near to tears.

"We'll discuss it at tea-time," he said patiently.

"But I have to ask you now! I don't know what you're thinking of doing between now and then."

He waited silently, and with some curiosity, until she was controlled enough to go on.

"Don't tell Rosamund," she said at last scarcely above a whisper. "I—she—I know you won't believe this, but please don't sneer at me now, for God's sake just listen to me and let me say it."

"I'm listening, Jane, and I'm not sneering. Say what you want to say."

"Don't tell Rosamund anything about it at all. She mustn't know. She's—"

The voice seemed to fail again. "She's not to be worried," said Jane firmly at last. "I won't have her worried. She's suffered enough. I want her to have a little happiness. I want her to—I'd *die* rather than have her know or even guess!"

"I promise you that Rosamund shall know nothing," replied Robert more kindly than he had believed he could ever speak to Jane again. "My love to your mother. See you. Goodbye."

Extraordinary, he thought as he put the receiver down; I believe she really does care for Rosamund in some weird sort of way. But then so did the girl in the book. It wasn't just straightforward cold-blooded villainy. In a way that made it all the worse. Poor Jane. How scared she had sounded. The girl in the novel had not been afraid. But then her man, although earning his living, had been on the fringes of the upper-class drawing-room society, subscribing to its ethos of keeping human passions more or less politely concealed. Some sort of nineteenth-century gentleman. Very different from a late twentieth-century bastard foundling, nobody's child, not bound by any social rules, with an experience of life quite alien to the well-mannered and self-controlled little drawing-room world.

It had been wise of Jane to remove herself last night. There had been a few minutes of real danger.

Raymond Quick's flat was on the first floor of a new block overlooking Regent's Park. He explained to Robert that his daughter was always urging him to go and live with her and her family in Devon, but their ways were not his ways, and as long as he was healthy and active he preferred to do for himself. And, of course, there was Rosamund to be thought of. He would not dream of leaving London while she was alive.

"I'm sorry to say she's not too good this morning," he said in answer to Robert's enquiry. "Some sort of stomach upset. No immediate cause for alarm. Mrs. Patterson told me on the telephone a little while ago, but of course in Rosamund's condition even a very minor trouble has to be carefully watched . . . No, my dear boy, it is certainly not the result of her walk in the garden yesterday. Of course that tired her, but this is something quite different. And even if there had been any bad reaction to her exertions it would have been worth it. It gave her great joy. I'd never thought to see anything give her such joy again and I'd like to thank you."

"You won't thank me when you've heard what I've got to say." Robert took a drink of coffee and then held out the book he had brought with him. "Have you ever read this novel?" he asked.

"*The Wings of the Dove* by Henry James." Mr. Quick flipped through the pages before returning the book to Robert. "No. I've not read it. I watched the television serial of another of his novels some time ago but I know nothing about this one. I'm not a great reader. Music's my thing."

"Then I'll tell you the plot as briefly as I can," said Robert, "and go on to tell you as briefly as possible why it is connected with Rosamund and myself and then I'll explain what I want to ask you to do."

Mr. Quick listened in silence. A clearheaded and competent young man, he thought; goes straight to the essentials, doesn't waste time upon unimportant details, sticks to the point and doesn't hesitate.

When Robert said, "And what I'd like to ask you to do," Mr. Quick interrupted him.

"I am going to fetch you some brandy. I think you need it. And I do too. This is one of the most extraordinary things I have ever heard. I feel sure you are right, and that this is what Jane has had in mind, but it has quite shocked me."

When he came back with the brandy he was taken aback by Robert's appearance. He was leaning back in the chair with his eyes closed and looked really ill. When he began to talk again there was no more calm exposition. He sounded pleading and desperate.

"If she talks of leaving me any money you've got to stop her. I can't bear it. I couldn't have borne it even before, and now I've discovered this—you've got to stop it."

He drained his glass, rubbed a hand across his eyes, leaned back again and said: "I just can't bear it. I love her. All I want is to help her to be a little happier. I don't want any money. I never think of the filthy money." His voice rose and with a great effort he got it under control again. "I feel sick with it all. Sick and ashamed."

"My dear boy." Mr. Quick leaned forward in his eagerness and touched him on the arm. "You must not feel this way. You have done nothing wrong at all. On the contrary, you have been the unwitting tool—but you have now found out and you have a chance to do something about it. Let me try to think calmly. I am quite convinced, and I am sure you must be too, that Rosamund has not the slightest suspicion of this scheme of Jane's, and provided nobody gives her *The Wings of the Dove* to read there is no reason why she ever should have. She did mention to me that she thought Jane might be hoping for a legacy, but that is nothing unusual. If she wants to make a little present to Jane we must not try to dissuade her. That might indeed arouse some suspicion. From Rosamund's point of view, therefore, Jane's scheme has so far brought nothing but good. Jane did her good, and now it has brought her you."

"And you call that a good?"

"I most certainly do. You have brought her light and warmth when all the rest of us had failed. It's not Rosamund about whom I am worrying at the moment. It's you."

"Me?"

"Yes. You are the chief loser."

"I suppose I am," said Robert. "I hadn't thought of it that way. I just feel ashamed. And I also feel a stupid credulous fool!" he added vehemently.

"That's better. Go on being angry. It will do you good."

"I've been feeling so guilty towards Jane because I felt so drawn to Rosamund—I do love her, Mr. Quick. It sounds crazy, so suddenly like that, but it's true and real and quite different than with Jane. And there I am feeling guilty and all the time Jane is crowing with triumph! I'm playing into her hands. I'm doing exactly what she wanted."

"Clever," said Mr. Quick. "Jane Bates is a very ingenious young lady. I wonder whether she would have thought up such a scheme on her own, without having read the book?"

"Oh, she got it from the book all right. And she'd have got away with it too if it hadn't been for my American student."

Mr. Quick sat thinking for a little while. At last he said: "Do you know, Robert, I cannot help wishing that Jane had got away with it? You look shocked, and indeed I am quite shocked at myself. But after all, supposing you had never read that book? You would never have suspected Jane's scheme. You would have brought Rosamund happiness. She would have left you a large sum of money and you would have accepted it because you would have known that was what she wanted. You would have mourned her death and Jane would have comforted you, and the two of you would have been united in love and gratitude to Rosamund, and if her spirit could look down on you, it would certainly feel delight at the sight of the pair of you enjoying her generosity."

Robert began to protest. "You can't deny," Mr. Quick

went on, "that such a result would have made for satisfaction all round, except perhaps in the case of Rosamund's relations, but they don't deserve to be satisfied."

"Do you mean to say," demanded Robert, "that you don't see anything wrong in Jane's scheme?"

"Not at all. I think it is immoral and repulsive. Human beings should not try to play at being God. I am only saying that it could have had something like a happy ending. But it's a very good thing you have found out," went on Mr. Quick hastily after a glance at Robert's face, "and I will try my best to do what you ask. It's no good begging you to forget all this when you see Rosamund again, because obviously you can't, but I do urge you to try to remember that she knows nothing about it, and try your best to behave as if you know nothing about it either."

"It's ruined everything," said Robert gloomily.

"No, it hasn't. You can still make Rosamund happy. I would have suggested that you come with me when I go to Willoughby House this afternoon, but I think two visitors would be too much for her. Suppose I ring you this evening, and then if she is well enough we can go together tomorrow? Everything will look very different then."

Robert got up to go. Mr. Quick added: "Don't be too hard on Jane. I can't help admiring her, you know. Whatever her faults, she is full of courage and of life. It would be very sad if she ended by losing both you and the money."

"The whole business makes me sick," said Robert. "But thanks for seeing me. And tell Rosamund—"

"I shall not tell her you have been to see me. I shall say that you telephoned me to ask me to give her your love."

"Oh yes. That would be best." Robert paused at the door

of the flat. "You're quite sure she's all right?" he went on. "I mean, that she's no worse?"

"Quite quite sure," replied Mr. Quick. "I had a long conversation with Dr. Milton on the phone just before you came and he assures me that she has weathered this little upset very well and is now resting and will be fit to see me later this afternoon."

If Robert had been less preoccupied with his own discoveries he might not have been so readily convinced by Mr. Quick's assurances, but as it was he simply repeated his message to Rosamund and said that he would look forward to hearing how she was as soon as Mr. Quick got back from Willoughby House.

After he had gone Mr. Quick took out the file of documents that he had been studying before Robert arrived and made a long call to one of the partners of his firm, a fellow trustee of the Morgan estate. When that was done he rang Willoughby House and spoke to Mrs. Patterson.

"Much better," she said in answer to his enquiry. "Dr. Milton is very pleased with her."

"Do you think she would be able to talk to me now?"

"I think it would be better if you would leave it for another couple of hours. She's sleeping at the moment and I'd rather not wake her."

"You don't think I ought to come straight away?"

"Well," began Angela Patterson slowly and doubtfully.

"All right," said Mr. Quick. "I can tell that you think I would only be in the way. Tell Dr. Milton from me that he has until exactly half-past three to get Rosamund into a fit condition to talk to me."

After he had replaced the receiver Mr. Quick leaned back in his chair and decided that it was not a bad thing that he had this enforced respite. He needed to conserve his strength to carry out Rosamund's wishes and to take whatever further action needed to be taken about the present situation at Willoughby House. That phone call from Nurse Patterson early this morning had been quite a shock, and he had been just beginning to reconcile himself to it when Robert arrived with his extraordinary story, and that had shocked him in a rather different way. What a good thing it was that he had been able to say perfectly truthfully that Rosamund had not named him in her will! Mr. Quick was very nearly certain that later on today he would not be in a position to make such a statement. Of course he would do what Rosamund asked, but he could foresee all sorts of problems piling up for the future.

As he sat there relaxing in his favourite armchair, he noticed that Robert had left the paperback copy of *The Wings of the Dove* lying on the coffee table. Mr. Quick picked it up and began to read. There was nothing else urgent to be done and it would pass the time.

He found it very hard going. But I'll get through it somehow, he promised himself. Curiosity was very strong. Not that he disbelieved Robert's story. It answered all his own doubts and questions about the little red-haired nurse and made sense all round. He still loves her, though, in his way, thought Raymond Quick; otherwise he would not be so very angry. Rosamund is a kind of dream. He will suffer very much when she dies but he will recover. And if what I suspect is going to happen really does take place, what will be the end of it? What will the young man do when actually faced with the temptation of great wealth? And what will the little redhead do if she is driven into a corner and forced to choose?

Love and money. The old lawyer had seen much of the effects of both forces during his life, but he could not remember ever having seen them in such dramatic and fascinating conflict before.

He picked up the book again and struggled on, cursing the author's style but becoming drawn into the lives of the characters in spite of himself, and sat reading until it was time to go to Willoughby House.

9

"I'm sorry," said Jane. "I can't say any more."

She too looked as if she had had a sleepless night. They sprawled in their usual armchairs and drank tea. Fury on one side and dread on the other had given way to an overpowering sense of flatness and gloom. They bickered, but there was no life or spirit in it.

"You're not sorry at all," said Robert. "You're just annoyed at being found out."

"Well, it was bad luck, wasn't it, about your American student. You'd never have suspected otherwise."

"And that would have made it all right, I suppose. The only crime is to be found out."

"There wasn't any crime!" cried Jane with a little flash of her old self. "That was the beauty of it."

"Beauty," repeated Robert with weary disgust. "Using human beings as pawns."

"We're all being used as pawns in one way or another all the time only we don't know it. And it's not usually to such good effect as this would have been. If it had worked out everyone would have been happier and no one would have suffered. It was so beautifully neat. You ought to appreciate that. You love a neat solution to a chess problem."

"But can't you see anything wrong in it at all?" asked Robert despairingly.

"Not really. Not if it had come off. People are always introducing people to others and hoping they will like each other and even fall in love with each other. What's the matter with that?"

"But this wasn't just a question of more or less innocent matchmaking." Robert, too, showed a flash of his earlier outrage. "It was loaning me out, like some sort of bloody gigolo, to get hold of a fortune that you hadn't got the nerve to get hold of yourself. It's like—it's like—supposing it had been the other way round, and you'd been my wife, and I'd hired you out to some rich old man—well, that's a crime to start with. It's called living off immoral earnings."

"But that's quite different," said Jane.

"Why?"

"Because." She hesitated. It was the first time that she had not been ready with an answer. "Because I do truly care for Rosamund and I was hoping that you could make her happy."

"And it would have been quite all right if I had truly cared for the old sugar-daddy and was hoping that you could make him happy?"

Jane turned her head and buried her face in the cushion. Robert fetched more tea. When he came back she had recovered a little and she said very quietly: "In any case, I'm a loser too. You really do love Rosamund. If she were to get well you'd leave me tomorrow."

"It'd be your own stupid fault," retorted Robert, but the sting had gone out of his voice again.

"So what are we to do?" she asked presently. "Do you want me to clear out? Shall we break up the flat? Or shall I go back and stay with Mother for a bit until things have calmed down?"

She looked small and pitiful and defeated. Mr. Quick's last words came into Robert's mind: don't be too hard on her.

"What do you want to do yourself?" he asked. "We can go on as we have been doing if you like. Being polite to each other. I can stand it if you can. If Rosamund dies we can think it over again. She's worse, by the way." And he gave Mr. Quick's report.

Jane seemed genuinely distressed. "I ought not to have left her," she said. "I'm sure I could get her over this."

Robert was beyond being astonished. It really did look as if Jane was going to ask for the job of nursing Rosamund again.

At the same time as Robert and Jane were deciding their immediate future or, rather, letting it drift on without coming to any decision, an informal conference was taking place in Mary Warley's sitting-room at Willoughby House between Mary herself, Mr. Quick, and a short, plump, fair man who held his hands behind his back and every now and then rose on tiptoe as if seeking to obtain greater height. The other two were sitting down.

"Are you suggesting," said Mary Warley very stiffly, "that I am not telling you the truth when I say that the only drugs I have given to Rosamund during the last twenty-four hours were the two sleeping tablets?"

"I am suggesting nothing of the sort," said the short man impatiently. "All I am saying is that her present symptoms might well have been caused by an excessive dose of analgesic or sedative and that Nurse Patterson says that there are six or eight fewer tablets of Prednesol left in the bottle than there ought to be. As you no doubt are aware, in excessive doses it is a stomach irritant, causing nausea and haemorrhage."

"Perhaps she gave Rosamund too much by mistake."

"She says she didn't."

"There you are then, Dr. Milton. You are clearly implying that I gave her the tablets. I do not know how I am supposed to have done so without her consent. Rosamund is neither a child nor is she senile. She likes to know what medicines she is taking."

"Surely there could be other explanations," interposed Mr. Quick. "Nurse Patterson might be mistaken. Perhaps somebody took the tablets for their own use. Or perhaps Rosamund took the additional tablets herself. After all she is by no means bedridden, as she demonstrated herself yesterday."

"Has she got a key to the cabinet?" Dr. Milton addressed Mary.

"I don't know," she replied. "I've never asked her. It is, after all, her own house."

Dr. Milton once more raised himself on his toes and said nothing.

"Has anybody asked Rosamund whether she took any tablets?" asked Mr. Quick.

Apparently nobody had.

"Then is there any objection to my asking her myself?" he continued.

"I will come with you," said Dr. Milton.

Mary Warley stood thinking for a few minutes after they had gone and then went downstairs and opened the door to the left of the front entrance. Rosamund's father had used this room as a library and working-room and Bill Warley had taken it over. As Mary had expected, he was sitting there now, in the chair at the desk, apparently writing.

He did not look up as she came in and she moved forward silently across the deep-pile carpet. As she came closer she saw that he was covering sheets of paper with calculations, a favourite occupation of his.

"And how much of the Morgan estate have you disposed of this afternoon?" she enquired sarcastically.

"Damn you, Mary." Hastily he pushed the sheets of paper under the blotter. "Why d'you have to creep about like that?"

"You heard me come in. You're scared. That's all."

"Why should I be scared?"

"Because of your foolish, clumsy, and utterly infantile attempt to kill Rosamund."

"I don't know what you are talking about."

"Rosamund is sick today. We have been over everything that could conceivably have been responsible for it. Dr. Milton thinks it is due to an overdose of Prednesol, Nurse Patterson says that there are at least six or eight tablets missing, and they are accusing me of having taken them. Do you wish to join in the chorus against me?"

"Of course not," said Bill, looking everywhere in the room except at Mary. "Perhaps Ros took the tablets herself, poor kid. She gets a lot of pain sometimes."

"That possibility is at this very moment being investigated. Will you kindly tell me, before Dr. Milton confronts me with the information himself, what it is that Rosamund might be able to tell him that would give him a clue?"

There was no reply.

"I'm waiting, Bill," said Mary.

"How should I know? I've nothing to do with Rosamund's medicines."

"But John Aylmer has a key to the drug cabinet. And after our talk yesterday you and he decided together that it would be better for you to have it, being in the house. It was safer that way than trying to steal my key, wasn't it, Bill? If my key was missing, then I wouldn't be the obvious suspect, as I am now. Would I?"

"I don't know how you can think up these things," said Bill. "You've always said you've got no imagination."

"It doesn't need any imagination to understand the truth. Some time after Nurse Patterson had gone last night you went to the nurses' room and took some of those tablets out of the bottle. It must have been when I was on the telephone. You know that when Mother phones I'm liable to be stuck for the next half hour. How did you get her to swallow them? Did you tell her you'd brought her a cup of tea? Or what?"

"I haven't done anything," said Bill. "I didn't go to see Ros at all last evening. I've told you. And she'll tell you too."

Mary continued to question him and his denials became more and more feeble.

Outside the door of Rosamund's room Dr. Milton spoke to Angela. "How is she?"

"Rather better. She's very anxious to see Mr. Quick."

The two men glanced at each other. "I'll go and check and then leave her with you," said the doctor. "I'll be in the nurses' room if wanted. In any case I'd like another word with Nurse Patterson."

He was back in a minute, saying that Rosamund was definitely improving but not fit to discuss any business matters. Mr. Quick looked down at the briefcase that he was carrying. "I think she'll find the strength to deal with this," he said. "You'll both be here, will you, if I need you?"

The doctor and the nurse exchanged glances. The lawyer opened the door of the room and went in. The curtains were drawn across the windows and the only light came from a reading lamp that stood on Rosamund's desk. Some sort of scented spray just triumphed over the smell of sickness and disinfectant.

Mr. Quick put his briefcase down on the floor and placed a chair near to the head of the bed.

"Here I am, my love," he said. "Take your time. Tell me as slowly as you like."

"Ray." Her hands moved over the sheets and she turned her head slightly on the pillow. "Have you got all the documents?"

"Everything that's needed."

"Then this is what I want to do."

Forty minutes later Mr. Quick was sitting with Dr. Milton and Nurse Patterson in the nurses' room.

"I'll stay on for the night," said Angela firmly. "I wouldn't dream of leaving her now."

"Then we'll have her in the clinic for blood transfusions tomorrow," said Dr. Milton. "I'd rather not move her tonight."

"I wish she would stay in hospital," said Mr. Quick.

"It would certainly simplify my job," said Dr. Milton, "but I've no doubt that she'll want to come home if she picks up again."

"You think she will pick up again?"

"She might. A little. After the transfusions."

"But for how long?"

The doctor shrugged. "Your guess. My guess. Anybody's guess. At any rate you appear to have removed the motive for hastening her death. Are you going to let her relations know that the best chance of a substantial legacy will be to keep her alive in the hope that she will alter her will again?"

"I shall go and see Mrs. Warley in a minute or two," said Mr. Quick. "I have the feeling that she will be very anxious to speak to me."

"But you don't think," began Angela Patterson.

"I do not think she would harm Rosamund, however great the temptation, but I think she knows more than she has told us. Will you leave me to deal with it, Dr. Milton?"

"Most willingly. The whole business is extremely disagreeable."

But you make a great deal of money out of having Rosamund as a patient, thought Mr. Quick, and even though you don't get a legacy, you receive a very large cheque in settlement of your final account when she dies.

"I'll be going then." The short plump man got to his feet.

"Incidentally," said Mr. Quick, "I think we may have the answer to the mystery of how the tablets were administered. Rosamund said she woke in the night feeling thirsty and took a long drink of orange juice. She was half asleep and went to sleep again almost immediately, but she seems to remember that it tasted bitter."

"That could be it," said Dr. Milton. "The tablets are soluble."

"But the orange juice," said Angela frowning.

"I'll leave you people to get on with it," said the doctor and hurriedly departed.

"Who gives her the orange juice for the night?" asked Mr. Quick.

"I used to when I was here," said Angela. "But last night it would be Mrs. Warley, only I don't see why—"

She broke off, looking very unhappy.

"I agree that it doesn't make sense," said Mr. Quick. "Mrs. Warley is experienced in nursing. If she wished to ensure that Rosamund did not live long enough to change her will she would make a better job of it. Is that what you were thinking?"

"Yes."

"Could it be done, without rousing Rosamund's suspicions, absolutely safely and certainly and without fear of detection?"

"The best way would be by injection, intramuscular," murmured Angela. "Dr. Milton has given her just now a 30-mg dose of diomorphine for sedation. Double—no, to be quite sure, quadruple, that dose would kill her."

"But would it be detectable?"

"The post-mortem would establish it, but it might not be so easy to fix the responsibility on to anybody."

"Why?"

"Because there are several of us nursing her. If it were between Mrs. Warley and myself, for instance, we should each blame the other, and if we stuck to it, which of us would be believed? It couldn't be proved. There is absolutely no way of proving these things if people stick to their stories."

"You frighten me, Mrs. Patterson, but I fear you may be right. The question of proof is always a stumbling-block. Let us hope that it won't come to that."

"You're not suggesting that I, Mr. Quick—"

"Heaven forbid. And thank heaven you are here tonight. No, I don't think that you are capable of killing anybody." He looked at her closely. A fine, intelligent face; well-cut grey hair; a neat figure in the nurse's uniform. "Except perhaps a true mercy killing. Yes, I think you might just be capable of that. And I should like to think that I would be too."

He stood up. "We are getting morbid. And I am getting fanciful. I have heard so many strange things today, and it has been a very long day but not finished yet. I must go and try to bear some of the burden of Mrs. Warley's conscience now."

10

Mary Warley, having long since finished with Bill, was waiting in the front hall. Bill had taken himself off, possibly to report his failure to John Aylmer and ask his advice, but more likely, thought Mary, to seek comfort at the pub.

"Could you spare me a moment?" she said to Mr. Quick. "We could go in here."

She indicated the door of Benny Morgan's library, now Bill's sanctum. It was a sign of her distress that she did not, in her usual regal fashion, summon him to her own sitting-room upstairs.

"How is Rosamund?" she asked first of all.

"Improved. She's going into hospital for blood transfusions tomorrow."

"Thank God." Mary sat down in one of the leather armchairs and motioned to Mr. Quick to do the same. "I've found out exactly what happened and I will tell you everything," she went on.

Mr. Quick composed himself for yet more listening. He seemed to have been doing a lot of it today. And yet his talk with Robert felt as if it were a very long time ago. Poor Robert. He would have to be told of Rosamund's condition. The day's tasks were not yet over.

"I'd left Rosamund's glass of orange juice, covered, on the draining-board in the nurses' room," Mary was saying. "It had been in the fridge and I was leaving it to get the chill off before giving it to her. He dropped the tablets in then, while I was in with Rosamund settling her down for the night."

"Thank you for being so frank with me," said Mr. Quick.

"I have no alternative. There is hardly any need for me to say what I feel about this. I can't make any excuses or any apologies. We are entirely in your hands." Her glance fell on the briefcase that Mr. Quick had placed on the low table beside his chair, and she flushed. "You had business for Rosamund to attend to?"

"I will be almost as frank with you as you have been with me, Mrs. Warley. It is not exactly professional, but the circumstances are such as to warrant a breach of trust. Your cousin has dictated to me an amendment to her will. With two witnesses available, we were able to execute it. I cannot tell you exactly what the changes are, but I will tell you that it would be to Mr. Warley's advantage, and to that of Mr. Aylmer, to do everything that they possibly can to please her and to regain her trust during the time that is left to her."

Mary looked away. After a moment's thought, and still not looking at him, she said: "You refer to my husband, not to myself. Am I to get nothing?"

"No, Mrs. Warley, *you* are not to get nothing."

The emphasis on the "you" was not lost on Mary. The flush deepened until her whole face became a blotchy red.

"Thank you," she said at last.

"There has been a certain adjustment, but the allowance made to you for running this establishment will be considerably increased during the rest of Rosamund's life. It will take effect immediately."

"Thank you," said Mary again.

She seemed to be speaking with great difficulty. Mr. Quick thought he had never seen her so near to losing her self-control.

"I can't tell you any more," he said, "but I think this may help you to deal with your own problems. And for your own sake, as well as for Rosamund's, we think it would be advisable for you not to undertake any more nursing duties when she comes home. Mrs. Patterson will take on as much as she is able, and Dr. Milton will arrange for two retired nurses whom he knows to do the rest. So there will be no need to have any more agency staff. And the lock on the medicine cabinet will be changed."

"What about meals?" asked Mary very quietly. "I do most of the cooking. Would you like the nurses to prepare Rosamund's food? There is a gas ring in their room. I could easily arrange for a small electric cooker to be installed."

"That's very thoughtful of you," said Mr. Quick kindly. "I will ask Dr. Milton what he thinks. And now I think you must be very tired. I know I am." He stood up and picked up the briefcase.

Mary stood up too. "And my husband?" she asked faintly.

"I don't think there is much good to be gained by taking any action against him at the moment, do you? After all, any official investigation could only be very distressing and damaging to Rosamund herself, and our main consideration must be to spare her in every way possible. Don't you agree?"

Her assent came in a barely audible whisper.

Jane answered the telephone. "Could I speak to Mr. Fenniman, please?" said Mr. Quick.

"Can I take a message? He's fast asleep. He's terribly tired."

"I'm sorry to ring so late, but this is the first opportunity I've had. Perhaps I'd better ring in the morning."

"Couldn't you tell me instead? It's Mr. Quick, isn't it? You'll remember me I expect. Jane Bates."

"Of course I remember you. It's not very long ago, is it?"

"Is she all right?" The voice sounded nervous and anxious. "Rosamund—I mean Miss Morgan."

"What makes you think she isn't all right, Miss Bates?"

"I don't know. I'm just afraid—"

The voice sounded suspiciously near to tears. Another of them, thought Mr. Quick. If I don't get to bed soon I'll be weeping myself.

"Miss Morgan has not been very well today," he said calmly, "and she will be going into hospital for blood transfusions tomorrow. You are a nurse yourself and you will know what value to put upon this information in the case of such a patient."

"Thank you for telling me," said Jane quietly. "Shall I tell Robert?"

"Please. That's what I'm ringing for." He was about to ring off, but Jane was speaking again.

"I wish I could see her. Will she be coming home again? I'd love to come and nurse her."

"And I'm sure she'd love to have you, but I'm afraid it's all been fixed up."

"Oh well. Perhaps I could come and see her some time. Goodnight."

Mr. Quick spent two or three minutes wondering what Jane was up to now and what Robert had said to her, and then he went to bed and was almost instantly asleep. Jane did not return to bed. From being as exhausted as Robert had been, she was now very wide awake. Was this really just a routine blood transfusion, or had Rosamund taken a turn for the worse? How was she going to find out what was going on at Willoughby House? Was there any chance of salvaging anything from the wreck of her plans?

The talk with Robert had been every bit as bad as she had feared and for a little while she really had felt that she would never long for riches again. But after he had calmed down and they had decided not to do anything drastic just yet she had felt a little better. Nothing he had said, much though it had hurt her at the time, had really convinced her that she was in the wrong. If she were willing temporarily to lose him, when she loved him so much, for the sake of greater good to come to them both, then nobody could accuse her of being selfish and incapable of sacrifice. And provided Rosamund did not know of the scheme, Rosamund herself could surely not suffer for it.

The only part she was willing to concede was that Robert might be justified in feeling he had been made use of. But surely the fact that she herself was taking the terrible risk of losing him cancelled that out. After all, Kate in the novel had ended by losing her man. Robert had read it now and knew how the story had turned out. Obviously he was furious at having been duped, as he saw it, but he hadn't actually walked out on her. And the fact that he felt guilty because of the way he felt about Rosamund was a weapon in Jane's hands if she could only find some way to use it.

The more she thought, the more she became convinced that all was not lost. The one essential factor—Rosamund's feeling for Robert—was still present, probably stronger than ever. Had he not believed that she was thinking of making him her heir, he would not have been so angry, but would have laughed the whole thing aside. It was his own consciousness that made him so wild, and no doubt it would drive him to try to prevent this happening. But this would defeat its own end, because it would be further proof to Rosamund of how much he deserved it. That she distrusted her relations and would like to benefit a more worthy inheritor Jane had discovered for herself.

Jane's natural optimism reinforced her reasoning. Whatever she had set in motion would continue now without any action on her part, and she must keep herself in the background, letting Robert think that she was very sorry and was trying hard to reform. She would start by being very economical over the housekeeping, since it seemed that they were to continue to live in the flat together for the time being. She might even ask his advice about opening a savings account. And never ask him about Rosamund but take her cue from him. Kate in the novel had failed because she tried to dominate her young man completely. Jane would not make that mistake, and maybe she would end up with the glittering prizes after all.

During the following days Robert felt grateful to have a heavy programme of teaching at college, and Jane's unobtrusive presence at home was not unwelcome. They departed early for their respective jobs, chatted about little incidents in the day's work over their evening meal, and spent most of their spare time reading. When the telephone rang for Robert, Jane took herself off to the kitchen and shut the doors in between so that she was out of hearing. It cost her a great effort to do this, since she was dying to know what he and Mr. Quick were saying to each other, but it was no good doing things by halves. She was playing for very high stakes and must stick to her role.

In fact the conversations would not have told her much that she did not know already. After a brief medical report, as satisfactory as could be expected, Mr. Quick said that Rosamund had asked him to give Robert her love and that she was looking forward to seeing him when she got home.

"Can't I visit her in hospital?" asked Robert.

"She would rather you didn't. She says she doesn't want to think of you in connection with hospitals. She asked me to say to you one word—'grass.' She said you would know what she meant."

There was no arguing with this. But he had another question. "Mr. Quick—it's all right, isn't it? About what I asked you? There's no danger—you won't let me down, will you?"

"I assure you that I have constantly in mind the request that you made when you came to see me that morning," replied the lawyer. "By the way, you left your copy of the Henry James novel with me."

"I know. I had to buy another."

"Then may I keep it? I find it very fascinating."

"Do keep it," said Robert. A new thought struck him. "Is Rosamund likely to read the book?"

"Unlikely in the extreme," replied Raymond Quick. "She prefers history and biography to fiction, and she's hardly likely to have the stamina to get through so solid a tome at the moment. I am sure you can put your mind at rest on that score."

How strange, thought Robert. It was as if he had always known her. She was a vision, an image that had been with him all his life, and yet he didn't even know who were her favourite authors.

"What can I bring her when she gets home?" he asked. "I'd like to welcome her back with a gift of some sort, and it would have to be a book or something she can look at. Flowers or plants? I thought you might have some idea."

There was a perceptible pause before the reply came over the wire.

"Do you know, it is most extraordinary," said Mr. Quick, "but in all the years I have known her, which is in fact her whole life, I think this is the very first time that anybody has consulted me about a present for Rosamund."

"You mean people think she has so much already that there's no point in giving her presents?"

"I don't know what I mean." The old man sounded quite distressed. "I only know that nobody has ever asked me that question before and I don't know how to answer it."

"Then I'll have to think up something for myself," said Robert.

From thenceforward all his waking hours, when he was not obliged to be concentrating on something else, were taken up with thoughts of a present for Rosamund. Flowers were too obvious, books were too heavy, clothes of any sort were irrelevant, perfume didn't appeal to him. He very nearly bought an ivory chess-set, knowing her genuine interest in the game and thinking they might make use of it together, but the thought that she might be too weak for such an effort of concentration deterred him.

A ring? No. Too full of symbolism. Some other sort of jewellery? No. Whatever sense in that for a dying woman?

Some sort of game or toy would be best. Simple but attractive and interesting. He spent forty-five minutes in a shop selling a variety of computer games, but could find nothing that satisfied him. Certainly they would amuse

Rosamund and pass the time, but they didn't seem right. They smelt of the future in which she would have no share. Rosamund's thoughts must be fixed on the present and on the past; she must have a gift from the past.

So it was back to the antique shops again, and it was in one of them, in a side street near the college, that his search came to an end. The shop specialized in Victoriana, and the object that caught his eye was a mahogany musical box with smooth rounded brass corners. It played four tunes, among them "Drink to me only with thine eyes."

A cheerful-looking girl wearing a floor length brown cotton dress, and with her hands perpetually going to her head to repair an elaborate but disintegrating hairdo, let him play with it for some time.

It was delightful. Had he been lying ill in bed Robert felt that it would have given him great pleasure—the smooth wood, the tiny effort required to turn the handle and select the tune, and the music itself. Rosamund must surely know the words of the Ben Jonson poem. If not, he would remind her.

His current bank balance, augmented by the full monthly limit of his credit card, just covered the payment. It gave him a great feeling of satisfaction to give out all he had.

"I'd rather not take it with me now," he said to the girl who was repairing her hairdo yet again. "Could you hold it for me till tomorrow afternoon?"

He did not want to leave the musical box with the secretary at college for safe keeping, since it would be bound to cause some gossip. Still less did he want to risk its being seen by Jane. Not that she was likely to show any sign of curiosity in her present mood, but to bring the box under the same roof as Jane seemed to him wrong, just as it would have been wrong to give Rosamund a computer toy. The musical box must go straight from its present resting-place into Rosamund's own hands and unless he heard from Mr. Quick to the contrary, that would take place at about five o'clock tomorrow afternoon.

Rosamund was being brought home today.

"Give her twenty-four hours to settle in," Mr. Quick had said, "and Nurse Patterson will be there tomorrow, so you will see a familiar friendly face."

The whole of Robert's life seemed to have been working towards this one moment when he would bring his offering of devotion to Rosamund. It was as if all the murdered hopes and expectations of his own childhood, that he had struggled so hard to suppress and deny, had come to life and merged together into this overwhelming sense of the anticipation of joy. Part of him drew back and looked on with amazement and fear. It was insane to set your heart and hopes to the task of building up such an edifice. The possibilities for disappointment were infinite, beyond imagination. The having dared to fall in love with Jane was nothing in comparison.

11

She accepted his gift with such wonder and joy that it was as if he himself were receiving a blessing.

She insisted on holding the musical box on her lap as she lay propped up in bed and her fingers caressed the smooth wood.

"What does it play?" she asked.

"Four different tunes, but there's one in particular that I like. I'll set it, shall I?"

"And you wind it up like this?"

The handle turned easily, the little effort was well within her strength. She raised the lid and they listened together. He looked at her face and it was indeed like feasting with the gods.

"Shall I put it on the table?" he asked. "It's heavy for you to hold."

"No. Let me keep it." She closed the lid and stroked the wood again. "Oh Robert. Oh Robert."

Presently she asked where he had found it. He described the shop and the girl who couldn't keep her hair up.

"If I had been given only one moment of life to live," she said, "and could choose which moment, this is the one I would choose."

Again they remained silent, out of time.

"Have you read Marcus Aurelius?" she asked. "My favourite philosopher. The stoic. He's great on the fact that you only live moment by moment and when you die you don't part with all life at once, but only with that particular moment of it, just as you've had to part with all the others that have gone before."

"I shall never part with you," said Robert.

"My dearest, you must. You're thinking that I look better. I'm not. I'm only flushed with someone else's blood. They won't be able to do it for much longer. One can't exist on other people's blood for ever."

"I wish you could have all of mine."

"Then you'd be dead and I alive. What good would that be?"

"Perhaps we could share it."

"Two half-lives? Oh, don't let's talk any more about blood. What an ugly-sounding word it is. Tell me what you've been doing while I've been away. I don't think you've been very well. You look strained. You've acquired some lines in your face."

She raised a hand to smooth them away.

"I'm all right," said Robert. "If we're going to talk I'd been rather hoping for a different topic for today."

"Such as?"

"Your favourite authors."

"I've just quoted one of them."

"Tell me others."

She mentioned a few names, but interrupted herself to say: "Robert, you're not happy. You're worrying about something. Take the box—yes, put it here where I can see and feel it. That's right. Now look at me."

She held his face between her hands.

"There's something very wrong. Is it Jane?"

He could not look into her eyes and deny it.

"I was afraid so," she said. "Will you tell me?"

"Can I tell you next time? I'd rather not spoil today."

"Nothing can spoil today."

"But by next time it'll probably be all sorted out," he said.

"You mean you two are going to part?" She spoke with quick anxiety. "I think you had better tell me now. Next time may be too late. Have you quarrelled over me?"

"Oh, why can't we forget Jane and just think of ourselves!" he cried.

"Because that's the way it is. Because she loves you. Because you're going to need her—terribly badly you're going to need her—after I'm gone."

For answer he laid his face down on her hands as he had done at their first meeting.

"All right," she said. "We won't talk about it now. But promise me one thing—that you won't quarrel irrevocably with Jane."

"I promise," he muttered.

"And now you must go. Come again very soon. And pull the table nearer—I shall play with my musical box after you've gone. Thank you again, Robert. My own dearest Robert."

Angela Patterson accompanied him to the front hall. There was no sign of the other inhabitants of Willoughby House. But it was very different from the last leave-taking of her.

"Try not to be hopeful," she said.

"You mean she's worse?"

"They did tests in hospital—the results weren't good. I had hoped, a little while ago—but all the faith and fight seems to have gone out of her again. Damn them," added Angela with unwonted violence.

It was not clear to whom she was referring, but it didn't seem to matter very much.

"Come again very soon," said Angela.

When he got home Jane took one look at his face and said that she was just going out. She'd left him something to eat, but she had promised to join a gang of them from the hospital who were celebrating somebody's engagement. Robert did not believe her, but did not say so. He put some cold meat and salad on a plate, placed it on the cleared corner of the table in the living-room, and sat down and looked at it listlessly.

If Nurse Patterson had given up all hope then this really was the end, because she had been the most optimistic of them all. Moment by moment. Yes, of course you only lived moment by moment, but this meant that you had to suffer afresh, every moment, the prospect of losing Rosamund.

Robert picked up the plate, took it out to the kitchen, and put its contents back in the fridge. Economical habits were second nature to him. Jane, in such circumstances, would have thrown the food in the rubbish bin.

The thought of Jane brought its own peculiar type of ache. He almost wished she were not so tactful, so terribly careful not to distress him. To explode in anger against Jane would at least be some relief to his feelings.

You'll need her when I'm gone, Rosamund had said. Suppose she were to die tonight? A sick panic seized him at the thought. Then the image of her playing with her musical box came into his mind and he could hear her thanking him. The sickness receded, but he could not work nor read.

When Jane came in very late she found him slumped in a chair and she felt a moment of panic herself.

He stirred. "Very tired," he muttered. "Going to bed."

Jane lay awake for many hours. This could not go on much longer. Robert was at breaking point. And she herself, determined though she still was to fight to the end to turn her dream into reality, scarcely knew how she was going to stand it. It was as if she was split into two people. One of them lived in the dream; the other was shot through and through with pain at the sight of Robert's love for another.

So the days passed. Every evening Robert was at Willoughby House. Sometimes Mary Warley opened the door to him and in spite of his preoccupation he noticed that she looked old and ill. They exchanged a few words about Rosamund and then she left him. He never saw her husband or John Aylmer.

In the nurses' room the changeover would be taking place. One of Dr. Milton's elderly ladies briefing Nurse Patterson on the condition of their patient. And he would find Rosamund caressing her musical box.

Sometimes the magic moments came to them. Sometimes they just sat silent, clasping hands. And sometimes they talked. She led him to talk about Jane, with such tenderness and loving understanding that he did not realize how much he was giving away. The details of Jane's plot she could not know, but the essence of it filtered through.

"Poor Jane," she said several times. "I hope you will never leave her."

He was grateful that she did not exact a promise. He could not cope with futures and finalities.

When he left the house Angela Patterson came with him to the door and answered his mute enquiry.

"I can't tell you how long. Nobody can know how long."
"I wish—"
"Yes, I know. Goodnight, Robert."

There came an evening when they scarcely talked at all, but played the musical-box tunes through several times.

When Robert and Angela Patterson came away from the room he could not look at her with his usual appeal, but grasped her hand with both his own, turned his head aside, cried, "Please, please," in an agonized voice, and hurried out of the house.

Angela returned to Rosamund's room and waited while the melody from the box tinkled to an end.

"Mrs. Patterson?"
"Yes, my love?"
"You know what I would like you to do?"
"Yes. I know."
"Will you do it?"

There was only the briefest hesitation before Angela said: "Yes. I will."

Rosamund closed her eyes. Her breath came in short gasps. She held up a hand to show that she wanted to speak again.

"I don't want you—to be blamed," she said at last.

"I promise you that I will not allow myself to be blamed," said Angela.

Rosamund turned her head and held out her hands. Angela sat on the edge of the bed and grasped them.

"Do you believe in God?" asked Rosamund.
"Yes," was the reply.
"Do you believe that what I am asking is right?"
"Yes, because you are asking it to spare the man you love, not for your own sake."

Rosamund's fingers gripped convulsively. Presently she was able to speak again.

"And do you believe that you are right to say yes?"

"I know that I am right in saying yes," said Angela.

"Thank you. Kiss me goodnight."

"Goodnight, my love."

Some hours later the middle-aged woman in the starched nurse's uniform was kneeling by the bed, her hands covering her face, whispering to herself: "God forgive me, please God forgive me."

After a while she got up and turned the table lamp towards the girl lying in the bed and examined her closely. The eyes were closed, the expression of the face was happy and peaceful and without pain. Nurse Patterson was about to draw the sheet up over the head, but changed her mind. No. Let her be found like this. Beautifully at rest.

She smoothed the sheet and arranged the hands over it. Then she bent over and kissed the cold cheek, straightened up again, drew her fingers across the smooth mahogany top of the musical box and left the room.

In the nurses' room she sat down at the Formica-topped table and began to write, noting the time at the top of the sheet of paper.

"Dear Dr. Milton," she began, and ended with: "You will find me at my home address, which I give below. I have no intention of running away."

She placed the key of the medicine cabinet on top of the sheet of paper, put on her coat, picked up her handbag, and left the room. In the corridor she paused to think. To undo the front entrance of Willoughby House would cause a certain amount of noise. The same applied to the back door. And then there were those burglar alarms at both the front gate and the tradesmen's entrance. She thought she could remember how to switch these off—after all, she was a sort of night watchman during these hours. It was the getting out of the house unheard that was the problem. Luckily she had come by bus tonight; sometimes she drove herself, at other times she did not want to be bothered with London traffic.

Perhaps the french windows in Rosamund's room would be the best way. Unlocking and unbolting them would make a noise, but the occupant of the room would not hear. Of course she could not secure the windows again from outside, but the risk would just have to be taken, she thought, suddenly impatient. What did it matter if a thief did succeed in getting through the outer defences? The only thing of any value in that house was gone for ever.

The night was very still, the grass soft under her feet. At least she had her walk in the garden, thought Angela. A stinging in the eyes and a feeling of great weakness were warning signs of her own inevitable reaction. I must get home quickly, she thought, and try to rest: I don't want to be in a state of collapse when they come to arrest me.

Mary Warley came into the nurses' room to tell Nurse Patterson that her breakfast was ready, but found nobody there. There was no coat on the hanger and the door of the medicine cabinet was wide open. She picked up the sheet of paper on the table and read the letter. Amazed and disbelieving, she read it through again, glanced at the syringe and the empty containers, touched her forehead as if she felt a headache coming on, and walked into Rosamund's room.

For a full minute she stood at the side of the bed, looking down, with the letter held in one hand and the other hand pressed against her temple. The pain was becoming unbearable, flaring up behind the eyes as if they were going to burst. She ran back to the hall, still carrying the letter and hardly knowing what she was doing. Bill's voice calling from upstairs forced her into some sort of self-control.

"Breakfast in half an hour," she called up to him. "I've got some phone calls to make."

She ran back to the nurses' room. Dr. Milton's number. She could use the phone in here. She lifted the receiver, began to dial, changed her mind and put the receiver back. "No, no, no," she muttered to herself. "Can't I do anything? Can't I save her?"

Burn the letter? Would Dr. Milton suspect that the death was anything but natural? After all, it was only to be expected, though perhaps not quite so soon. The headache rose in a crescendo. Mary Warley collapsed onto the chair. Not Dr. Milton. Not yet. She lifted the receiver again and dialled Mr. Quick's number.

When he arrived at Willoughby House twenty minutes later she was waiting for him at the front door. She caught his arm and dragged him along to the nurses' room, thrust Angela Patterson's letter at him and sat down by the table, putting her head down on her arms. The tears came out at last, slowly and painfully, like a mechanism creaking into action after many years of disuse.

After a while she raised her head, wiped her eyes, and saw the old man sitting opposite her as if stunned.

"Do we have to give this to Dr. Milton or tell anybody else?" she asked. "Can't we just—"

"Destroy it and hope that he will sign the death certificate? If you wanted it that way, Mrs. Warley, why did you not act for yourself instead of calling me?"

"I don't know. I suppose I knew that I ought not to."

"Not only that, but it would be useless. Mrs. Patterson would only write the letter over again or make her confession in person. We cannot, we have no right, to try and take over her conscience for her."

"No, I suppose not."

Mr. Quick surveyed the blotched face and untidy hair of the woman opposite him and felt a twinge of pity.

"I sympathize with your feelings," he said. "May I say that I am glad that you feel that way?"

Mary wiped her eyes again. "It seems so cruel and so unjust that she, who thought only of Rosamund—"

Her voice failed.

"Try to think of it as her own wish and her own decision," said Raymond Quick gently. "Do not make comparisons. You have done your duty towards Rosamund. Try to remember that."

Mary put away her handkerchief. "Would you like to see her? She looks very beautiful."

Together they stood looking down at the dead face, the old man and the grey-haired woman.

"I'll go and ring Dr. Milton now," said Mary at last.

"Perhaps you'd like me to do it for you," said Raymond Quick, "and stay and talk to him when he comes."

"Oh thank you. Thank you so much."

"And perhaps we could have some coffee while we are waiting?" He managed a faint smile as he said this.

"Oh yes. Of course." She looked at him gratefully and went off to the kitchen with an air of purpose, taking the first steps towards restoring her shattered image of herself.

12

Mr. Quick spent much of the morning at Willoughby House. He then went to the office and spent a long time with the fellow trustees of Rosamund's estate. After that he returned home and telephoned Robert's college. The switchboard operator promised to give the message as soon as he came out of his class. When he rang back Mr. Quick simply said that he was sorry he had bad news for him, and would he come round to his flat instead of going to Willoughby House that evening.

"She's dead," said Robert immediately.

"My dear boy, it's what we have been long expecting."

There was silence. Then Robert said: "Thank you for telling me. I'll be free in an hour. Please may I come round at once instead of waiting till later?"

"Certainly. I'll expect you."

And that doesn't give me long to try to decide what I'm going to say to him, thought Mr. Quick as he replaced the receiver. But perhaps it was just as well, because after all, what could he say except the truth? The death of the Morgan heiress would be in itself a news item, even though long expected and with no unusual circumstances. And if it came to court, which in the end of course it must do, well, he could see the newspaper headlines already. A human interest story like that would be drained to the very last drop.

So he would have to tell Robert everything. Instead of rehearsing his speech to him, Mr. Quick found himself going over in his mind that extraordinary morning at Willoughby House, from the moment when he had been greeted by the distraught Mrs. Warley to the moment when he had watched Dr. Milton's Mercedes bump off over the rutted lane.

Would Dr. Milton succeed in persuading Mrs. Patterson to change her story? Because that had been the upshot of that totally irregular, most extraordinary discussion between the lawyer and the doctor, two eminently respectable professional men doing their best to find a way of hushing up a murder. Because murder it was, according to the law of the land.

"If only she'd given something orally," groaned Dr. Milton.

"Yes indeed," said Mr. Quick. "So that Rosamund could have taken it herself. She could not have given herself an injection?"

Dr. Milton shook his head. "Out of the question."

"But in any case there's the letter. Would we be willing to suppress the evidence?"

"Oh damn the letter!" cried the plump little doctor. "Why the hell did the woman have to put it down in black and white like that? Has she got a martyr complex, or what? And why the hell didn't Mrs. Warley burn it when she found it, as she says she very nearly did?"

"Because she couldn't face the responsibility. She had to shift it, just as you and I are trying to do now. We're cowards, all of us. The only one with the courage of her convictions is Mrs. Patterson herself."

"She's got courage all right."

"She's shamed us all."

"Maybe that's what she wanted to do?"

The two men stared at each other.

"I don't think so," said Mr. Quick at last. "I think she just wanted to help Rosamund and to make sure nobody else was suspected of having done it."

Dr. Milton picked up the letter again and read aloud: "'I have taken this action, being in my right mind and fully aware of what I am doing, in order to spare my patient from any more of the intense pain and distress under which she is now suffering, not only the physical distress, but the mental pain of feeling herself to be such a burden upon those whom she loves.' What d'you make of that? She can hardly be referring to the girl's cousins."

"No," said Mr. Quick. "She means Robert Fenniman. That's why I'm quite sure that Rosamund asked her to do it."

"She doesn't say so."

"She wouldn't."

"In any case it makes no difference in law."

The discussion went round in circles yet again. At last Mr. Quick said: "One of us will have to inform the Public Prosecutor. Will you do it?"

They stared at each other yet again. Dr. Milton appeared to come to a decision. "Don't do anything until I've seen her," he said getting up. "She'll have to go off the Nurses Register, of course, but if we can only find some way of leaving it at that, without a trial—"

"Is there any way?"

"I don't know. Leave it with me for the present. I'll go and see her now. She's not a beneficiary, is she, by the way?"

"She gets nothing except a piece of furniture."

"And the cousins?"

"Mrs. Warley rather less, Mr. Aylmer a very great deal less, than originally intended."

Dr. Milton whistled. "Charities?" he asked.

"Also very greatly reduced."

"So the bulk of the estate goes to—?"

"Exactly," said Mr. Quick.

Dr. Milton whistled again. "You've got a job there. I don't envy you. Well, I'll be off to see if I can do anything at all about this other aspect of it. I'll ring you this afternoon or evening."

The call had not yet come, and it was now nearly five o'clock. Raymond Quick could only assume that Dr. Milton's efforts to do something had failed, as they were bound to do in the end. If Mrs. Patterson was determined to be accused of murder, nobody could stop her. Weariness overcame him. He was too old for this sort of thing. Rosamund was gone, freed from all her pain, and his task was over. Let the others deal with their problems for themselves.

He was dozing in his chair when the bell rang. It was a great effort to rouse himself.

"You must be very busy," said Robert. "I won't stay long, only I couldn't talk on the phone. How did she die?"

He appeared calm enough on the surface. Mr. Quick was relieved. Perhaps after all the worst of it could be postponed until tomorrow.

"Very peacefully," he replied. "Some time during the

night. No struggle. No pain. Just as we have been hoping. And as she has been hoping too."

"You don't mean she killed herself?"

"No, not exactly."

Mr. Quick was disconcerted. He had not intended the young man to leap to the truth in this manner; he was to be gently guided into it. But then Robert was a disconcerting person, and he ought to have realized that by now. What on earth would he do when he learnt the rest of the truth? The prospect of having to deal with him was quite dreadful.

"How do you mean, not exactly?" asked Robert.

"Nurse Patterson helped her."

Mr. Quick began to feel as if he were in the witness-box, awaiting the next attack from a relentless cross-examiner. When he had answered all the questions he waited in considerable anxiety for Robert's final reaction. It might be violent fury against Nurse Patterson. With this extraordinary young man one simply could not tell.

"Thank you for telling me," said Robert very quietly. "I should like to thank Mrs. Patterson. I had a sort of feeling that she might perhaps do something soon, but I never thought she would be quite so brave. May I have her address?"

Mr. Quick gave it. The whole business seemed to have been taken out of his control and he felt past caring.

"I'll leave you in peace now," said Robert getting up. "I'm sorry to have taken up so much of your time. But there's just one thing I should like to be reassured about."

They were in the hallway. Robert had his hand on the door as if wanting to be sure of his means of escape.

"It's not easy to say, but I'm sure you'll understand. You remember I asked you not to let Rosamund leave me anything in her will? Well, all I want to say is that if you didn't manage to persuade her, and if she did insist—"

He paused. He seemed to be rapidly losing his control. Mr. Quick could think of nothing to say. He could only wait.

"Then I don't want it!" shouted Robert. "I don't even want to know. You can do what you like with it. But don't tell me. I just don't want to know!"

He tugged at the door and then recoiled. A woman was standing in the corridor.

"I'm sorry I didn't use the intercom," she said, "but I found the front door open downstairs."

"Come in, Mrs. Patterson," said Mr. Quick. "You're the very person Robert wants to see."

"And I want to see him," she said. "That's one of the reasons why I've come. To get his address. And to seek your help, Mr. Quick. Dr. Milton has been talking at me so much that I simply can't think straight any more and it's not the sort of thing you can discuss on the phone. So I came along in the hope of finding you here."

At least there was nothing artificial about her calm, as there had been about Robert's. She looked tired, but as steady and reliable as ever. It was odd, though, to see her out of her nurse's clothes and wearing a very elegant light spring coat. Mr. Quick felt himself shrinking at the thought of yet more talk. On the other hand she had saved him from an impossibly difficult situation. What on earth was he going to do with Robert? Perhaps she would help him.

"I'm going to make us some refreshments," he said, his spirits rising at the prospect of pottering about the kitchen by himself for a little while, "and leave you two to talk."

Twenty minutes later he carried a tray into the sitting-room and found Angela Patterson alone.

"He's just gone," she said. "I thought you wouldn't be sorry."

"Far from it. I can only thank you. My sympathy and respect for that young man is very great, but I find him more than I can cope with."

"I know." She smiled. "There's something elemental about him. Larger than life. It's rather like being confronted with the passions of a Romeo or a Hamlet but without the protection of the footlights in between."

"How right you are." He poured the coffee. "When you arrived so opportunely just now, he was informing me in no uncertain terms that if Rosamund had left him any money he just didn't want to know. In view of the fact that he is principal heir to the Morgan estate, you can imagine my dilemma."

Angela laughed. "He's been dealing with me in like manner, trying to persuade me to evade the consequences of my own action."

"You won't be persuaded?"

"Mr. Quick, I did not do what I did on impulse. You once said to me that you believed me capable of a mercy killing. I was a little surprised at the time, but on reflection I discovered that it was true. I thought about it a great deal. My conscience is clear and I have no fear of the consequences. The only thing I do fear is that somebody may try to fudge the issue."

She's as bad as he is, thought Mr. Quick. The quiet middle-aged woman and the larger-than-life young man. What a terrifying thing it was, this passionate conviction. He had never thought of himself as either good or bad. He had loved and he had done his duty, but he knew that never, not even if he were granted his eighty years of life over again, could he either take it upon himself to release a human soul that was crying out for release, nor reject a fortune if it was offered to him.

"I'm sure Rosamund wouldn't have wanted you to suffer," he said tentatively.

"I have done what I could for Rosamund. It's a matter of what I want myself now."

"At least you will allow me to arrange for the best possible defence?"

"By all means. I've no wish to spend longer in prison than I have to."

She sounded so balanced and so sane. Perhaps she was. Perhaps it was all the others, the great mass of frightened doubters and conformers who were not. She didn't even ask what the penalty was likely to be, any more than Robert would ask the sum of wealth that he was rejecting. What a pair. Well, he supposed it made some sort of ultimate balance, two people's self-sacrifice against the cruel cutting short of one girl's life. He would do the best he could for her; she might get off lightly with a sympathetic jury, and then he would retire to Devon. The other trustees could look after the estate. But there was still a task to be done.

"Mrs. Patterson," he said, "since you have so much more courage than I have myself, I am going to ask if you will once again put your head in the lions' den and tackle Robert Fenniman for me. He is hardly likely to hit you on the jaw, which I fear he is quite capable of doing to me. Will you tell him about his inheritance and explain that if he is serious about not wanting it, he is perfectly entitled to reject it, but there are a number of formalities to comply with and I shall be obliged to ask him to co-operate."

"I'll do it gladly," she said, "provided I'm still at liberty."

"They will arrest you when I have made my report. You will be charged and later allowed out on bail. I will arrange that too. You'll have until midday tomorrow."

"Aren't you going to get into trouble for not having reported me immediately?"

"Yes, but I'll have to put up with it. It's nothing like the trouble you are in. And Dr. Milton must look after himself. And now may I please give you the details about Robert's legacy?"

He handed her pen and paper and she made notes. "Suppose," she said at last, "that he would like to make it over to another person. It's a possibility, isn't it?"

Mr. Quick groaned. "It is indeed. That beastly, beastly novel!"

Angela looked puzzled.

"I'll explain another time," he said hastily. "In that case it would be comparatively simple, provided the other person is willing to accept the gift."

They stared at each other.

"I assume we are talking about the same person?" said Mr. Quick.

"I think so," said Angela. "Rosamund confided in me a lot. Perhaps not everything. I don't know anything about a novel."

"It doesn't matter," said Mr. Quick. "I'm quite sure it will end differently. Life has its own surprises that fiction doesn't know how to imitate."

"You think he's going to offer it?" said Angela.

"Don't you?"

"I suppose he'll have to do something about getting rid of the money if he's absolutely determined not to take it."

"I tell you, that young man scares me. His feelings don't run between the normal well-defined lines. Any girl who takes him on has got to have great courage and great wisdom."

"Rosamund had both," said Angela gently.

"Yes." Mr. Quick was silent for a moment. "But it's somebody else's job now," he said briskly, "and I find that my curiosity about human behaviour is after all not at an end. I know in which household I should like to be a fly on the wall over the next few days."

13

"Rosamund's dead," said Robert.

Jane said nothing. She had not been long home and had just finished changing out of her nurse's uniform after the day's hospital work. Had she made any comment at all, even an attempted expression of sympathy, Robert could have flung the next sentence at her: "And if you want to know if she's left me anything in her will the answer is that I don't know."

This sentence, and many variations on it, were simmering in his mind. He longed to blame somebody for Rosamund's death, and that somebody ought to be Jane.

It was Jane. If it hadn't been for Jane, Rosamund would still be alive. Rosamund had begged for release, Mrs. Patterson had said, because she could no longer endure seeing Robert so torn and desperate. It was Jane who was to blame, not the nurse who had acted only from pity and at great cost to herself.

But you could not attack someone who said nothing.

Without uttering a word she proceeded to cook a meal, cleared the table, laid places, put a plate with lamb chops and vegetables in front of him. To his surprise he actually found himself eating it. When they had finished she produced cheese and fruit and coffee and finally cleared away.

"I'll wash up," he said. It was the first word that had been spoken since his arrival.

"Thank you." She picked up the book that she had been reading and settled down in her usual chair.

In the kitchen Robert found relief in controlled and careful physical activity. For a little while it was almost as if Rosamund Morgan had never been. He repeated the phrase in his mind. It seemed to clear his head and give him a clue. Not even a memory: just a dream. More real and more beautiful than anything in waking life. To live in the dream, with all the world around unreal, and to keep his dream to himself. That must be his way.

It kept him going for the next couple of hours. He even managed to exchange a few sentences with Jane, who scarcely glanced up from her book but hardly turned a page. When the telephone rang he picked up the receiver and she heard him say: "Yes . . . yes, certainly. I'll meet you there at nine o'clock tomorrow morning."

She did not look up when he put the receiver down. A little later she said: "I'm tired. I'm going to bed."

Robert said nothing. The interruption had shattered his dream. He wondered vaguely what Angela Patterson could want with him and why she hadn't been arrested yet, but it all seemed quite unreal and the dream was unreal too.

Jane pretended to be asleep, but actually lay awake wondering and worrying. Wouldn't it have been better to have a flaming row at once? This silent lethargy was frightening. He was like a zombie. But he had taken that telephone call. Who was he meeting in the morning? Could it be Mr. Quick, with news of Rosamund's estate?

There was no way of quietening her racing thoughts, of calming her excitement. Poor Rosamund was released at last; Robert was in shock, but he would get over it. He must get over it. And whatever he felt about Jane herself, he was certainly not indifferent to her. Love or hatred, but not the indifference against which one could do nothing.

As for herself, she had never ceased to love him but she felt that only now, after all these years, was she beginning to understand him. That stoical placidity was just a mask. The adaptability and willingness to be led was equally deceptive. There was something much tougher, perhaps even something rather ruthless, underneath.

But Jane felt sure that she would be forgiven in the end. The enormous efforts that she was making to keep to his standards and not to give the least cause for offence must surely be rewarded. And if Rosamund had left him the money—well everything simply must come all right in the end. Robert might storm and rage and swear that he wouldn't touch a penny of it but he would have to give in. People simply did not turn down large sums of money when it came to that point. They might believe they were going to but in the end they didn't.

It was this waiting and not knowing that was so awful, but it couldn't last much longer now.

How could one go into a fury over having been left a fortune that one did not want when in the presence of a woman who was waiting to be arrested for a mercy killing?

"If only it would buy Mrs. Patterson a pardon or release," he said later to Mr. Quick.

The lawyer promised that he would do his best for her.

"I can't feel anything but grateful," said Robert. "I just can't think of her as having committed a crime."

"Nor I. And I too loved Rosamund."

"She wanted only to die. I knew it. I felt it that last time."

He seemed to be genuinely calm now. Mr. Quick no longer feared an explosion when they began to discuss Rosamund's will. Robert listened attentively, putting a question now and then, and when Mr. Quick finished he said: "I know exactly what I want to do, but I don't know whether it is legally possible."

"If you will tell me, I will try to advise you."

Robert told him. Mr. Quick thought for a little while.

"It isn't quite as simple and as clear-cut as that," he said at last, "but we might be able to make it appear so. Enough to serve your purpose."

"That's all that matters. We can sort out the formalities later on when we know which of the two courses of action is decided on."

"You are quite determined? I cannot persuade you to consider a third course of action?"

"I am quite determined," replied Robert.

In desperation Jane rang Willoughby House. She could not bring herself to telephone Mr. Quick for information. After all, Robert might be with him.

Mary Warley answered the phone and told her that Rosamund had died peacefully and painlessly two nights ago, but that there were certain circumstances that might make an inquest necessary. She could not tell Nurse Bates any more just now. The funeral? Mr. Quick was handling the arrangements; it would be best to get in touch with him. She was not unfriendly, but there was no getting any more out of her.

A call to the nursing agency was no more productive of

definite information, even though the woman in charge was always glad of a gossip.

The temptation to telephone Mr. Quick became overpowering. Jane decided to go out in order to resist it. There were two hours to kill until one o'clock, when Robert had said he would be back. She walked to the nearest bus stop and got on the first bus that came along. It would take her into the worst of the West End traffic, but at least that would pass the time.

At Piccadilly Circus she got off and waited for a bus going back. At a seemingly endless halt in Edgware Road she stared at a shop window full of cheap and ugly furniture and began for the first time to lose some of the optimism that had buoyed her up from the very first moment that she had conceived her magnificent plan and had kept her going even during that horrible evening when Robert had discovered it.

Edgware Road shops. Not the ones she would choose if ever . . .

Why was it that looking out at them, and going back on the bus to the little flat, was making her begin to believe that it would be never? What was the point of having such a dream and fighting so hard to make it come true, when at the very last moment, just when it looked as if it was within your grasp, the dream itself began to fade?

If only the bus would move on. Edgware Road was like a prison: the prison of cheap and boring everyday life. And it seemed to go on for ever. The dream was growing dimmer and dimmer. The sense of foreboding was becoming intolerable.

The bus moved on at last. Going home, thought Jane with

relief. And into her mind came a little picture of home and comfort and security.

And of Robert.

What was he doing? What was he going to do? The foreboding returned and quite blotted out the remnants of the dream.

As she got off the bus she saw him alighting from the one in front. They met at the corner of the side road and walked along the little cul-de-sac together. The neighbours from upstairs, walking in the other direction, greeted them and they replied. A train went by noisily as they approached their front gate.

"The traffic's hell this morning," said Jane.

"I know," said Robert. "Tea or coffee?" he asked as they came into the living-room together.

"Tea, please. I'm sorry, I haven't done any shopping."

"Doesn't matter. We can do it this afternoon. I want to tell you something now."

He was speaking from the kitchen in a slightly raised voice. They always did speak like this when talking from room to room. It's just like what it's always been, thought Jane. For a brief moment she felt reassured by Robert's kindness, comforted by the sense of everything being as it always had been; and then she suddenly felt stifled, the foreboding came back even worse than before, and it was as if she was stuck on a bus in a traffic jam in the Edgware Road for ever and ever.

Robert came back and handed her a mug. It was the Earl Grey tea, her favourite.

"I just couldn't talk last night," he said. "I must have been in some sort of state of shock. You see, Rosamund didn't die naturally. She asked Nurse Patterson to give her an extra injection."

"And she did?"

"Yes."

"Good God!" exclaimed Jane, pulled, in spite of herself, right out of her own preoccupations. "How did they find out?"

"Because Mrs. Patterson told them."

"She must be mad."

"In a way, yes. But a rather wonderful way."

"Of course one sometimes feels, when somebody's terribly ill and there isn't any hope—which of course there wasn't with Rosamund—but actually to do it—"

A pause, and then Jane added: "I'm sorry, Robert. I hope you do believe that I am truly sorry. For your sake, I mean."

"Yes. I believe you are. Thank you."

There was a silence.

"That's only part of what I wanted to tell you," said Robert at last. "I had to sort out something first about the other part. I've done this now and got it all straight with Mr. Quick and it's up to you to choose."

Jane said nothing. The sense of dread had taken her over completely. She felt so weak that she could barely hold the mug of tea. Robert was sitting in the other armchair, where he always sat, leaning forward slightly as he always did when studying a chess-problem and seeming, outwardly at least, as calm and placid as he used to be.

But looking older, much, much older.

"After you and I last talked about Rosamund," he said, "I went to see Mr. Quick and told him that I would like him to persuade Rosamund not to include me in her will. He said he would do this if he could, but he was not sure whether she would be persuaded. Apparently she wasn't. I've therefore told him this morning that in no circumstances can I possibly accept any of the money but that I should like a say in what should be done with it. He says that it is mine to do what I like with. I decided on two possible alternatives and I told him I'd let him know which was the one to be followed up after I'd had a talk with you."

The sense of dread froze to a certainty. Jane drank the rest of the tea, put the mug on the floor, and leaned back to listen to the death sentence on her dream.

"The first alternative," said Robert, "is that it should be divided among the charities which she names in her will, and I'll say straight away that this is the one that I infinitely prefer, from every point of view. The second is the one that concerns you. It is that I make the whole lot over to you as a gift. Mr. Quick doesn't know exactly how much it will be —there'll be death duties to pay and some more will be lost in making the gift but it will still be a very great deal. You would not be as wealthy as Rosamund was, but in the same sort of category."

He stopped and looked at her. Jane stared back and they remained thus for several seconds.

Then she said: "I take it that there's a condition attached to the second alternative?"

"Yes."

"Do you want me to guess what it is?"

"If you like."

"Then I would guess that I would receive the money on condition that—" She stopped, gave a little gasp, and continued: "On the condition that I spend it alone."

"I can't accept it," said Robert. "I can't accept any share in anything that is bought with it."

They stared at each other again.

"In other words," said Jane, "I can have the money or I can have you?"

"Yes."

"My God, you put a high price on yourself!"

Jane jumped up from her chair. The life had returned to her; her eyes were blazing; she looked all prepared to fight.

"I don't think of it that way," said Robert. "I just can't take any part in the spending of the money."

"You do think of it that way! You're doing this to get your own back. It's cruel, it's horrible, it's—it's—" Jane took a great gulp. "It's diabolically clever."

She sank down onto the arm of her chair and said more quietly, "To think I've lived with you all these years and never knew you could be like this."

"And I'd lived with you all these years and never knew you could be like—like what I found out when I read that bloody novel. So we are neither of us what we thought. No illusions left. Here we both are. What are we going to do? It's up to you to choose."

"So what happens if it all goes to charity? You and I go on as we are? Just the same as it used to be?"

"It can never be the same as it used to be. It would be different. Whether better or not would be up to us."

"How could it possibly be better, with you hating me because I'm not Rosamund and with me hating you for depriving me of a fortune."

"If that's the way you think of it then you'd better decide to take the money. I wouldn't have suggested the alternative if I hadn't believed that we might still have something to give each other in spite of everything."

"Do I have to decide today?"

"Do you think we can live in this flat with this between us?"

It occurred to Jane then, fighting desperately, searching everywhere for an escape, that he might after all not be serious in intention, and that this might be a sort of test, like an ordeal in a myth or a fairy story, and that if she passed it she might yet win all.

Or something, even if not all.

A compromise? Remind him that in his heart he had deserted her for Rosamund? No, that was no use. He'd only retort that she'd forced him to it, that that had been her plan. But there must be some other way to strike a bargain. What were they dealing in? Love and money.

No. Love *or* money. A common phrase, commonly used without thought of what it meant.

Whose love? Hers for Robert. Well, of course. Why else was she struggling like this? Robert's for her? But he loved Rosamund. Except—well, why had he put the other alternative at all if he really wanted them to part?

Her thoughts became more and more confused. If only she could have time. But time would not help. He was right in that. If she insisted on time he would take it as a decision. And walk out.

Love or money, love or money. All the things that they could do with the money. Always "they." Not herself alone. Alone—and rich. Like Rosamund. At any rate she would not be ill. But it was a cheerless prospect.

"Love or money!" she suddenly cried out loud. "That's what you're asking me to choose."

"If you like to put it that way."

"How else can I put it?" She jumped up again and raged

around the room. "How can I possibly have any choice when I love you, love you, love you!"

Her voice rose to a shriek. She was just then reaching the table on which lay the heavy glass paperweight. She picked it up and in a frenzy hurled it at him. Robert ducked his head and the paperweight went through the window. They cried out in unison as they rushed to the shattered pane together and clasped hands and held their breath as they watched the paperweight crash harmlessly onto the roadway. A second later a car drove past.

"That was a near thing," said Robert shakily. "It could have killed somebody."

"It could have been you," said Jane. And then, a moment later: "I'm going to be sick."

She made a dash for the bathroom. When she came back some minutes later, looking very white but more under control, Robert was speaking on the telephone.

"Here she is," he said into the receiver. Then turning to Jane: "I've just been telling Mr. Quick to go ahead with the first alternative. But there's something he'd like to tell you. Do you feel up to speaking to him?"

Jane wiped her forehead and nodded. She took the receiver and sat down on the arm of a chair.

"Yes, Mr. Quick?"

At first she listened in silence, still rubbing her left hand over her eyes and her face. Then the hand moved to the back of the chair and her fingers started picking at the upholstery, like a cat. She blinked and frowned as if her head ached too much to understand what was being said.

"A house?" she repeated stupidly. "Why should Rosamund leave me a house?"

The patient voice at the other end of the line explained again. Jane looked across at Robert. He had sat down in his usual chair opposite, and the much older-looking face was regarding her very kindly.

"Did you know that Rosamund had left me a house?" she asked in a bewildered voice.

"Mr. Quick told me yesterday. There's quite a lot of property included in the estate. Her father bought several houses and flats at one time. Mostly in central London. Mr. Quick said Rosamund remembered the conversations she had with you and she thought you would like this best."

Jane's fingers worked away at the stuff of the chair. "Robert's just explained," she said into the telephone. "But I don't know whether . . . it sounds lovely . . . we did talk about houses . . . but I don't feel I ought to accept anything from Rosamund!" she concluded with a rush.

Mr. Quick groaned. Then he said very firmly: "I will leave you two to argue that out by yourselves. Goodbye."

He replaced the receiver and leaned back, shaking his head. Life was indeed full of surprises. Heaven alone knew what was going to happen to that couple, but it certainly was not like the end of the novel. In fact it didn't look as if it was ever going to have an end at all.

ANNA CLARKE was born in Cape Town and educated in Montreal and at Oxford. She holds degrees in both economics and English literature and has had a wide variety of jobs, mostly in publishing and university administration. She is the author of sixteen previous suspense novels, including *Letter from the Dead*, *Game Set and Danger*, *Desire to Kill* and *We the Bereaved*.